Death Bloom

A Midnight City Mystery

David N. Alderman

Prologue

February 23, 1997

The cold east winds blew through the empty fields as moonlight cast its seductive glow across the furrows of dirt and dry ground. Such a sparse, open plot of land was becoming rare in Midnight City. Most had been tilled and crafted into buildings, universities, entertainment structures, or convenience stores. Out here, near the boundary lines of Midnight City, the land was free for the taking.

But why was the land open? Why had nobody laid claim to this piece of property yet? There had to be reasons, and those reasons—on the surface, at least—seemed suspicious. This is what Augustine Rose questioned as she drove the beat-up pickup truck across the bumpy dirt field. Midnight City—especially the suburban areas—was subject to strange and unusual happenings, even moreso to evil and malevolent entities. Did something live out here, away from the rest of the city? Did something or someone consider this land their home, and they just hadn't bothered to tell the rest of the residents of the city?

Augustine felt the engine slip as it misfired. The vehicle was overdue for a tune up. 300,000 miles did a number on a vehicle like this, but it continued to remain dependable for her. For now. She hoped it would continue to serve her well. She couldn't afford another car, not with the mountain of student loans she had accumulated at the university. She had managed to secure the botany masters she had been toiling over the last six years, but the price was more than she could responsibly handle.

The truck hit a stone embedded in the tilled land and caused the vehicle to swerve to the right a bit. Augustine tugged on the steering wheel and righted her course, gripping the outside of the car door as she hung her arm out the window. She cursed under her breath, hoping the truck would keep it together. If she broke down out this way, who would help her? Nobody. Nobody she would *want* to help her, anyway.

In reality, the only real threat she had out here, under the blanket of moonlight, was the Order, a cult obsessed with plants. In fact, Augustine surmised, they cared more about plants than they did human life. She only knew of the Order because of her own diligent research into the cults of Midnight City. The group was all about self-sufficiency, ruthless politics, and the preservation of priceless flora. They were probably the biggest threat—of the cults, that is—to Augustine's own endeavors. She was surprised they weren't out here, beating her to the punch.

Of course, maybe they *were* watching her. That was always a possibility. She had adopted the distinct suspicion over the course of the past few days that someone had been following her around town whenever she left her home. Shadows that trailed her to the grocery store, the pharmacy, the home improvement center.

She didn't really care though. Risks had to be taken in the name of botany. If they were going to do something sinister, they would have done it already. No, they were *watching* her. *Waiting* for her to lead them to something. Maybe to this. This was why she had taken special precautions on her way out here tonight to shake any tales she might have 'grown' over the course of the last week.

Augustine was convinced she was alone out here. At least,

for the moment.

The field went on for at least a mile, ending at a line of trees that served as a boundary line connecting Midnight City to the Wastelands beyond. She had no reason to go any further, so she slowed the truck and shifted it into PARK, cutting the engine. The truck made a horrible clunking sound, and she wondered if it would start again when it was time to head home.

Then she sat in silence. The night was late—at least eleven, and the air was cold and smelled of pine and cow manure. It was a sobering smell, something Augustine enjoyed due to the fact it was one she had grown up with living on a farm.

This land had sat, abandoned, for years. Nobody else had seen the value in it. But there, in the middle of the field, stood a patch of tall grass. Something in the middle of it glowed bright, but it's light was dimmed by the circle of grass surrounding it. Even from here, that beacon seemed to beckon her.

She opened the truck door, and the screeching sound the hinges made echoed through the moonlit field. She froze, hoping it hadn't attracted the attention of any beast or killer. Then she realized how foolish that thought was and stepped out of the truck. As her sneakers touched the hard dirt surface, she felt a sudden pulse of energy. It was as if something…called to her.

Augustine left the truck door open—in case she needed a quick escape, she told herself – and started toward the patch of tall grass. She traversed the uneven terrain between, using the moon's light to illuminate her path. She had to stop and skip here and there to avoid tripping on the large stones imprinted in the earth. She figured most of the rocks would have been kicked up during the tilling of the field, but she reminded herself that this field hadn't been toiled in a very long time. Whoever had tried to plant in it must have realized the ground was

3

not going to give up its life, and they probably moved on to other more abundant fields elsewhere.

As Augustine approached the tall grass, she felt her connection with whatever was there grow even stronger. She withdrew a small flashlight from the pocket of her cargo pants and shined the light on the blades of grass. They were blue in color—bright blue when shined upon—and looked soft. She wanted to touch them but wasn't sure what it was she was looking at. She knew nothing of blue grass existing in Midnight City. *What if it's poisonous?*

She pushed through the grass tendrils and moved inward toward the center of the patch. There, nestled in the center of its protective ring, stood a glowing white tulip. The light seemed brighter than the moon, and the tulip itself looked as healthy as any tulip she had ever seen. The curves of the flower's petals gave off an elegant form, sensual almost. She could smell the scent of the tulip, and it was intoxicating. Strange too, as it was middle of winter, a time when tulips were not known to bloom.

Augustine knelt down and examined the ground beneath the flower. The soil was soft, moist, and dark – probably rich in minerals and nutrients. She examined the soil the grass blades resided in, and it was the same. It all looked healthy and ideal for plant life to grow, answering her question as to how plant life like this could survive in a field otherwise deplete of resources.

She stood to her feet, turning the flashlight off. She allowed the glow of the tulip to engulf her, engulf the blue grass blades around her. The flower seemed to sing to her a song of acceptance. It had summoned her here—she was sure of it.

Augustine pulled her phone from her coat pocket and dialed her assistant's number.

"Augustine?" A young woman answered. *"Is something wrong? It's almost midnight."*

"Purchase the land east of Lorraine Hill."

"What? There's...I thought you said there was nothing there. We went together the other day. Don't you remember?"

"Purchase the land. Immediately. Make sure all of the contracts have me as the sole owner."

The woman's groaning on the other side of the phone was an annoyance, but Augustine fashioned herself to ignore it right now. She was too excited, too enamored by her find. If someone had come out here to explore this, they would have taken it for themselves. Someone might have pulled that flower up from its roots, destroying it. But now Augustine had the opportunity to protect it. To cultivate it. To nurture it.

There was the sound of rustling papers on the other line. *"The price on that land is—"*

"I don't care. Pay it."

"I know it's not my place, but you realize your funds are extremely limited? You don't even have enough in savings to procure that land. Where are you-"

"Use the other account. The one I told you not to touch."

"Isn't that someone else's—"

"Do it, please. Get those contracts to me to sign. Let's get this done in the next couple of hours."

"Next couple of hours? Really? It's almost midnight, Rose. You woke me up, and you want me to contact this landowner and wake him up too?"

"Do what I asked."

There was a long, irritating pause before the young woman replied. *"Alright. Yes, alright, I can do that. I'll have the contracts sent your way as soon as I have them."*

"Very good." Augustine disconnected the call abruptly and shove the phone back into her jacket pocket. She didn't even care if the truck ran. She didn't care about anything but securing that land for herself and her future.

5

Chapter 1

The alarm clock buzzed and blared, shimming itself across the small nightstand. It fell over the side, crashing to the floor while it continued to let out a harsh noise that cut through the peace of the morning.

"Shut up!" Harvey Elder groaned as he reached down to shut the infernal contraption off, but his hand missed the alarm and instead smacked a half-eaten bag of cheese puffs. He tried again, this time smacking his palm into the side of a beer can, tipping it over and causing it to vomit the remainder of its contents on the brown, already-stained carpet.

Harvey rolled to the side and tumbled out of the bed. His body fell on a variety of different wrappers and drink containers, and he groaned again as he opened his eyes and spotted the insubordinate alarm clock. He smacked it as hard as he could with his palm, and the alarm stopped mid-blare, letting out one last electronic whine.

"Finally. Piece of junk."

He slowly got to his feet, and then sat on the edge of his bed. The morning light pierced through his trashed blinds, another reminder that it was a new day. A fresh start. Another chance in this life he considered a prison.

He rubbed the stubble on his face and ran his hand

through his short brown hair. The worst feeling in the world, he thought, was first waking up. A new day brought new problems. New irritants. New reasons to not want to continue forward in this life.

The small apartment suddenly shook. "Stop it!" Harvey yelled as the 9:10 train sped past his window. The tattered blinds shook and then the entire rod holding them up fell off the wall, landing on the floor.

Harvey shook his head and rubbed his eyes. His body ached. His head hurt. He couldn't really remember what he had done last night. He remembered lying in bed, drinking. That was it. Apparently, he had also eaten his fair share of junk food. Cynthia had called him? No, *he* had called Cynthia.

He grabbed his phone off the nightstand and scrolled through the call log. He had definitely called Cynthia. Probably left a very stupid, very immature voicemail too.

He went to throw his phone on the bed when it suddenly rang. He looked down at the Caller ID and saw a number he had never seen before.

"Hello," he answered.

"Harvey Elder. As I live and breathe, you actually *live and breathe."* The voice was raspy and rough, most likely from years of smoking.

"Who is this?" Harvey stood to his feet. He liked to pace when he took calls, but his floor wasn't going to offer him that option today. His room resembled a junkyard more than it did a living space at the moment.

"You wanted employment. Right?" The voice seemed to be hiding a cough. The caller was sick with something.

"I'm listening."

"I have a woman who lives downtown. Wants someone to find her

7

missing necklace."

"C'mon, man. I don't have time for stupid scavenger hunts. Who are you, anyway?'

"A…friend…of yours gave me your number, said you were looking for work. Also told me to be surprised if you actually answered."

"Cedric? Yeah, he isn't my friend."

"Do you want the work or not? Help an old lady. Find some missing jewelry. Make some pocket change. Win, win, win."

"That's not a win, win, win. And my answer is no. When you have a real case for me, go ahead and send it my way. I don't have time to help old ladies find their missing trinkets."

"Well, you have my number if you change your mind."

Harvey disconnected the call and threw his phone on the bed. He felt the tension in his neck at the frustration of getting yet another call to find someone's piece of junk jewelry or their missing pet. When he ventured out into the entrepreneurial field as a private investigator, he thought he'd be called in to consult for the police department or have people hire him to find their missing loved ones. Instead, all he'd been getting for months were calls to hunt down objects of interest—mostly heirlooms, and search for missing cats. Why were so many cats going missing in Midnight City all of a sudden?

He stretched, listening to the joints of a forty-something-year-old crack, and then he moved through his morning routine: showered, dressed himself, ate a bowl of kids' cereal that had gone stale from the package not being closed tight enough.

An hour later, he slid his overcoat on and stared at the main room, shaking his head at the sight of the mess. He knew he had to clean himself up. Drinking the nights away and avoiding work—any work—wasn't going to get him very far. He reminded himself that searching for an old lady's necklace was conceivably better than flipping burgers at Patty Time. Conceivably.

Harvey left his studio apartment and ventured into the city. His errands of the day included depositing twenty-dollars into his bank account to cover the thirteen-dollar overdraw, picking up his suit from the cleaners, and picking up some microwave meals from the grocery store to last him the rest of the week.

As soon as he finished his errands, the day had moved into night. Harvey returned home, cleaned up a bit of the place, and microwaved himself a bowl of macaroni and cheese.

Before he could sit down to enjoy his dinner, his cell phone rang. He saw Cynthia's name on the Caller ID and cursed the world.

"Hello," he answered, a heavy sigh in his voice.

"You called me last night, Harvey. Again. What did I tell you about that?"

"I don't…I don't remember calling you. I'm sorry."

"Sorry? You left me a five-minute voicemail going into great detail about how much you hate that I'm with Gregory now. You're lucky I didn't let him listen to it."

"I said I'm sorry. I just…I miss you, you know? And I get weird when I drink."

"That explains why you're always weird. I told you that we're done. I left you weeks ago, and you need to learn to pick yourself up and create a new life for yourself. I do care for you, you know? But I can't be your crutch. You have to want a better life for yourself. Pull yourself together. If Gregory were to find out about your calls, I promise he'd have you thrown in jail, with a restraining order."

Harvey crossed his right arm across his stomach and stared out at the somewhat-clean room. *Baby steps*, he thought. *I made some baby steps today.*

"Find yourself some decent work. Refocus."

"I'm trying. Some guy offered me a job hunting down necklaces."

Cynthia scoffed at that. *"You're better than that. Much better. If you actually applied yourself, I'm sure you would make a great* actual detective. *You know, like you used to be?"*

"I don't want to work for others, Cynthia. You know that. Look, I just need time. Time to get things together. Maybe you and—"

"No, Harvey. No, you and I are done. Get that through your head. We're done. You need to move on. The only way you're going to make it through all of this is to accept that fact. I don't hate you, I just find that I'm not compatible with your…means of living."

He felt the sting of that last comment, but he brushed it off. She meant to say he was too poor to be with her, but she would never say that aloud.

"I'm sorry I left you another voicemail. I'll work on that."

"Thank you. Don't do it for me. Do it for yourself. Goodbye, Harvey."

Harvey listened to the phone disconnect and then set his cell on the kitchen counter next to his macaroni and cheese. Cynthia was right. He had to pull himself together. The drinking, the laziness, the inability to let Cynthia go. All of these were factors to his current failures. He just had to find a way out of it all.

At least it doesn't smell like a homeless man relieved himself in here anymore. Mostly.

Chapter 2

The ringing of the phone did little to actually wake Harvey from his deep slumber. It was the combination of the 10:25 p.m. train shaking his entire apartment, the ringing of his phone, and the beats of the upstairs neighbor's techno music that finally teased him from sleep.

Harvey shuffled his hand around the nightstand, looking for his phone. He managed to bump the alarm clock as it fell and crashed to the floor. Again. He found the phone, opened his tired eyes, and saw that no number was coming up on his phone.

"Hello?" he answered.

At first, there was no response on the other end. Instead, he heard light breathing and the shuffling of papers. Then a female's voice came on in a whisper. *"Mr. Elder?"*

"What time is it?"

"Time? It's...12:46 a.m."

"Why?"

"Why what?"

"Why are you calling me? I was sleeping." He sat up in his bed. The shaking from the train knocked his blinds down again (he had just reattached them before bed), and the streetlight just outside his window nearly blinded him.

"Mr. Elder, I don't have much time. I'm calling you because

I…we…need your help."

He rubbed his face, realizing he had forgotten to shave the day before. *At least the apartment is somewhat clean.* "With what?"

"I know you may think this silly or strange, but we need your help finding the thief of a priceless flower."

"You're kidding me."

All he could hear was shuffling papers for a few moments, before the woman finally spoke again. *"I'm not. Look, they don't know I'm calling you in. But I'm desperate. I don't know who to trust around here. I don't know what to do."*

"A flower? I'll pass."

"I'll pay you five thousand dollars to come down here and at least listen to the case. Another fifty thousand will be yours if you take and solve it…with discretion."

Harvey took a very brief moment to make sure he had heard the dollar amounts correctly. Fifty thousand dollars would at least cover his room and board for a good year or so. That would enable him to be pickier with his cases without having to listen to everyone give him grief about it. He could even take a break for a month or so and 'pull himself together' as Cynthia had put it.

"Who gave you my number?"

"A friend."

Cedric!

"Five thousand just to come hear you out?"

"Yes. Listen though, Mr. Elder. Nobody here knows I'm calling you down here. I have my own reasons for doing so. But I ask for discretion above all else. Five thousand, you come listen to the case. I can't explain it on the phone. You have to see it for yourself to…appreciate it."

Harvey took a deep breath as the train finished its passing of his home. In its wake, the thumping from his upstairs neighbor's music seemed louder, more pronounced. He would go up there and have a 'chat' with him, but that had already happened once, and Harvey had found himself on the receiving end of a knuckle sandwich. So, he let the man play his stupid music. Harvey would find a way to solve that problem through other means at another time.

"Mr. Elder. I need an answer if you please. I'm taking a risk just calling you."

"Where do you want me?"

"The Midnight Botanical Gardens."

"What time?"

"As soon as possible."

He grunted. "Fine. I'll be there in an hour or so. I just need—"

"You do know what as-soon-as-possible means, right? It means be here in twenty minutes. I'll throw in another thousand if you can manage that."

"Fine. I'll be there *shortly.* Who do I ask for?"

The other end had already hung up the call.

Harvey set his phone down on the bed. He sat there for a moment, listening to the drumbeats from above his head. The way they coasted through the ceiling, he wondered if any of his other neighbors could hear the music.

He wondered…if Cynthia would take him back if he could make something of himself. Yes, she could be materialistic and somewhat vain. But they had been high school sweethearts who came back into each other's life in the last two years. He loved her. She left because after he thought he had been responsible for a girl's death—and found out later that her mother had in fact killed her—he tried to return to detective work, and that didn't work out as he had planned. Cynthia wanted more than he could cough up in his state. He was a washed-up detective.

He had been content with that, as long as he had Cynthia.

But now she was gone too.

He did have to pull himself together. If not even for himself, then for her. He could show Cynthia that he still loved her. That he wanted the best for her. Maybe her desires weren't the most noble or right, but he knew, deep down inside, that she loved him.

Harvey stood up, stretched, and got himself dressed. He slid on his shoulder holster, slid his .38 Special into it, and then gathered his lockpick kit and fingerprint dust in case he needed them in his investigation. Then he headed to the Botanical Gardens.

Chapter 3

I t wasn't like Harvey to follow orders. Hard enough to follow them from his superiors. Much harder to follow them from a no-name caller requesting his investigative services.

To spite the woman who had called him—and to make sure he'd be able to stay awake through an entire early morning investigation—he stopped off at a coffee shop that sat on the route from his apartment to the botanical gardens.

Dark Grounds was a small independent coffee shop located on the last corner before reaching the Varintale Bridge that led out of the main city and into a more remote area where the botanical gardens existed within. The building itself was older—almost as old as Midnight City, and it had been repainted and remodeled a dozen times over the course of those years. It had cycled through multiple owners who tried their hand at running a coffee business only to be outdone by rising rent costs throughout the city.

Harvey was surprised the place still functioned as a coffee shop and hadn't been bought up by the city or some multi-million-dollar corporate snob.

Harvey stepped through the doorway into the small café.

Monique Ball, a quirky, 30-something female with the tenacity of a bartender, turned from sweeping a dust pile.

"Harvey?" Her short brown hair and the silver nose ring hanging between her nostrils for dear life conveyed a young countenance. But Harvey knew Monique was an old soul—possibly an older soul than he.

"Monique."

She leaned against the broom, wiping a hand on the brown smock she wore. "I'm closed, hon. All my machines are off for the night."

He nodded, then took a seat at one of the small tables. "For me? I have a case I'm on my way to. I'll throw in a nice tip."

Her face lit up, her hazel-colored eyes sparkling like fireworks. "A case?"

He nodded.

"A *real* case?"

He frowned. "Real case? What is that supposed to mean?"

Monique dropped the broom on the floor and made her way to the coffee pots behind the counter. "Geez, don't get so defensive. I mean, c'mon, you and I both know you haven't had a real case since…well, since the incident with Samantha Eves and her daughter."

Harvey scratched the stubble at his chin. "I know," he mumbled. He heard Monique start up a coffee maker. The drip sound and the smell of fresh coffee filled the room. He almost wanted to stay here, to forget about the botanical gardens. Who cared about a stole flower anyway?

"I don't mean anything judgmental by that," she said as she came out from behind the counter. Her thin frame moved with fluid motion as she made her way to his table and took a seat across from him. Harvey knew she danced in her spare time, down at the studio. She loved dancing as much as he loved detective work.

"You know I care about you, Harv. I've always believed in you. You're the finest detective I've ever known—even though I only know one, which is you. But still. You were born to do this stuff. You notice everything. You listen to everyone—even when they aren't speaking with their mouths. It's in your blood...despite what Cynthia tells you."

Harvey shifted in his seat. Cynthia. He couldn't recall once when Cynthia actually showed she believed in him and in what he did. Still, he loved her. Someone didn't have to love what you did for a living to love you. Right? But then he didn't know much about Cynthia's chosen profession, except that she dealt in insurance.

Monique leaned in close to him. When she spoke, her breath reeked of strong coffee. "Get yourself a woman who respects you. Cares for you. Loves you." She leaned back in the wooden chair and fiddled with the multiple gemmed rings adorning her slender fingers. He knew most of it was costume jewelry, but it brought a flash of color to her brown coffee wardrobe. "You're putting your life back together. Got your career going in the right direction. You ditched that creep—"

"*She* broke it off with me."

She pointed at him. Her nail, he noticed, was painted with splotches of purple, teal, and cerulean. "*You* ditched that creep and sent her packing. Now you can fill that hole with someone better."

"You have anyone in mind?" he asked, more as a joke than anything else. He had fantasized on a few occasions what it might be like to be with Monique. She was uncontrollable. Chaotic. Intelligent. Cute...lacking elegance, but more than making up for it with raw beauty that many women Harvey had come across in his lifetime just did not possess.

She smirked. "My friends are all out of your league. I mean

that in terms of their aspirations, nothing more. They want to drink, party, and sleep around."

Harvey motioned to the room. "You seem to be doing well for yourself."

She raised her eyebrows. "I have. Mostly. Keeping this place afloat with the rent increases over the last few months is making it a challenge. But yes, I'm different from my friends. I would rather build a future than drink my present under the table."

She tapped her nails on the surface of the table. "You have so much potential in you, Harv. I want to be there when you really shine, when you show those naysayers—such as Cynthia—that you have it in you to be a great detective." She stood up and started toward the coffee maker. "Because you do."

Harvey listened as she poured his coffee into a ceramic mug. She brought it to him, setting the cup down on the table in front of him. "Drink up. Go solve your case. Prove me right."

He leaned back in his chair, holding the warm cup in his cold palms. He heard rain coming down outside. A storm.

He watched as Monique picked up the broom and returned to sweeping.

"You have five minutes," she said. "I need to get home and get some sleep."

Sleep. While the world slept, he would be investigating a stolen flower. He sipped the coffee, allowing the strong liquid to slide down his throat. He was going to need the energy. Something told him this case was going to turn into something so much more.

The cases he always thought were going to be small always ended up offering the greatest challenge.

Chapter 4

B efore leaving Dark Grounds, Harvey did an internet search on the Midnight Botanical Gardens. He knew little to nothing about the place. He had never had any reason to visit, and he had never solved a crime that had any connection—as far as he knew—to the place.

Not to mention, he knew little to nothing about flowers, nor did he have any interest in them.

The Gardens, as they are commonly referred to, has been in existence since 1999. The center is a popular place in Midnight City—especially in springtime. In the winter, however, a normal botanical garden wouldn't bring in much of an audience. Not many plants bloom well or beautifully in the winter. Not enough, anyway, to justify keeping a center open weeklong.

The Gardens is different in this regard, in that it has some of the strangest exotic flora that seems to bloom and blossom year-round. Harvey heard one or two rumors of the Gardens before, usually from drug-addled informants on the street. They liked to ramble about supernaturally imbued plants— Haunted Plants, as they called them.

Harvey didn't believe in such things. Plants were plants. They weren't living creatures—not in the sense of humans or animals. Sure, they were technically living specimens, but they didn't have superpowers or personalities. Or haunted attributes.

Harvey finally said his goodbyes to Monique—a quick peck on her cheek and another brief speech from her about how he could do so much better with his life—and left the café. He drove across the Varintale Bridge through the winter rainstorm around 1:34 a.m. and entered the eastern quadrant of Midnight City. Mostly farmland and vegetation resided out this way, which is probably why the botanical gardens existed in this area.

With the rain came chilling cold that settled in for the late night. The chill left Harvey wanting to turn the car around and head back home to his bed. Or at least head back to the café and chat it up with Monique a bit more. He found her encouragement enduring. She genuinely believed in him and in what he did, and he found it both unbelievable and exciting that someone could have so much faith in him.

Because he had little faith in himself.

But that five thousand dollars was beckoning him. And that fifty-thousand dollars even more so.

He pulled his 1983 Datsun 200SX into the parking lot of the botanical garden's main building and parked near the front. The car shuddered as he pulled into the spot. The vehicle had served him well enough, but he knew it was time to upgrade. It had been an inheritance from his father after the man passed away three years ago from lung cancer. His dad used to joke that the car—much like Harvey—was too stubborn to fail. The frame was slightly bent, the radio would only play three stations, and the gears in the side mirror to his left had busted, making it so the mirror was permanently stuck in a loose, down position, giving a nice glimpse of the road itself. He had meant to make time to go to a junkyard to find another mirror, but when just cleaning his apartment became an insurmountable task, going to the junkyard felt like taking a trip across the sea.

Right now, the Datsun looked like an aged kids' toy compared to the handful of high-end vehicles scattered around the lot near him. Jeeps and convertibles. Even an Escalade. Already, he felt out of place. Most of the time, he felt that way anyway because of his car. Or his clothing. Or his ratty apartment. They didn't really put together a good picture of a man who had his life together and was successful.

He would change that.

Harvey turned up the radio volume and listened to "Don't Fear the Reaper," watching the rain splatter across his windshield. His car heater was broken, but he knew it was colder outside, so he chose to wait a minute before making the trek to the building. Besides, he didn't really know what to expect with this strange phone call. Who was it exactly who had called him? He realized he hadn't taken down her name. And why would she be calling him behind the back of those around her? All because of a plant thief? *Ridiculous.*

His phone buzzed, and he pulled it out of his pocket to check who would be contacting him at almost two in the morning. It was a message from the Midnight City Police Department, about a murder victim on the other side of the city. He frequently received these police alerts, thanks to a friend he had in the Department. The hope, at least to Harvey, was that with whatever little information he was given, he might be able to help the Department in some capacity solve a murder or a heist. Or something like that.

Crime Alert - Unidentified white male found dead in west end of Midnight City. Cause of death unknown. Victim found unresponsive on street and called in by passerby. Name on ID hard to read. More information to follow...

Harvey stared at the rain sliding down his windshield. A mysterious death? He would have loved to be on the west side of Midnight City right now, investigating that instead of pursuing a plant thief.

He put the message in the back of his mind and slid his phone into his pocket. Maybe he could wrap up this plant thief business and get to the west end of town in time to help out. Or he could take the five-thousand-dollars for simply *listening* to the case about the plant thief and then refuse the case and be on his way.

He nodded to himself, happy to have options. Happy to have control over something in his life.

The song ended, and some obscure ad for The Crystal Tavern blared twice as loud in his speakers. He killed the engine and bundled his overcoat. He felt like a slob, just throwing worn clothes on to venture down here. But he didn't have time to do laundry. Nor did he really have time to care about how he looked.

He reluctantly stepped out of the car. The rain smacked into him with prejudice as he slammed his car door and straightened out his overcoat. He looked up at the building. A pathway started from the parking lot and cut through an aisle of large plants before ending at double doors leading into the building.

As he made his way down the cobblestone path, lit by little lawn lamps that glowed softly under the pouring rain, he gazed up at the plants. He recognized them as Venus flytraps, but these were at least ten feet tall. *Someone fed these things Miracle-Gro.* Each was potted in a black ceramic base. They didn't seem to be moving, though he felt them watching him. Waiting, maybe, to devour him or any other unlucky trespasser to the botanical gardens.

When he reached the glass doors, he found them locked. Peering through the glass, he saw a massive lobby filled with leather couches and chairs, ornate coffee tables, and end tables with little lamps on them. A lone receptionist desk sat still, undisturbed, off to the side. In the very center of the room stood a small display case on an ornate pillar. Inside was a glowing flower. Various garden-themed posters lined the walls behind it. Double doors stood further beyond the desk, and he figured behind them were the actual botanical gardens.

The rain pelted him harder, as if it was actually out to get him and him alone. He went for his cell phone, but before he could retrieve it from his pocket, a slender woman appeared at the door and unlocked it.

"Sorry," she whispered, beckoning him inside. He stepped into the lobby of the building. She shut and locked the door behind him, and then turned to face him. "My name is Jessica Harper. I'm sorry to do all of this so secretively."

Harvey ran his hand through his wet hair and examined the young woman. She was about a foot shorter than he was but seemed a little taller thanks to black heels. She was slender—especially in the black skirt and white blouse she wore, had a beautifully crafted face, and wore dark-rimmed glasses that lent a sophisticated look to her overall elegant frame. She wore a white open drape cardigan that gave her a homely feel to balance the rest of her ensemble. Her long black hair fell across the shoulders of her blue sweater in a lazy way, as if her hair was the only thing she didn't apply upkeep to. Her eyes glistened a bright blue like pools of water, but they seemed full of suspicion. She was smart, he could tell this much right off the bat. Which begged the question of why she needed his help with a simple missing plant.

"Mr. Elder?"

He snapped out of his trance and cleared his throat. "Yes, sorry. Look, I don't mind the secrecy. I just need to know what's going on if you want my help."

She handed him a folded envelope. He could smell cherry blossom perfume on her person. "Here. There's six-thousand dollars there."

"Six?"

She nodded. "I told you I'd pay another thousand if you came quickly."

He laughed in his head. He had taken his sweet time getting here, and she thought he was quick?

He took the envelope. Figuring it would be rude to count the money in front of her, he crammed the envelope into the inside pocket of his overcoat, delighted to have some cash to his name again. Maybe he could buy a new set of blinds. Maybe a new alarm clock.

She looked up at him, her glare narrowing on his face as her nostrils twitched. "I'm sorry if this seems kind of rude, but have you been drinking?"

Harvey scoffed. "Does it matter? No. But does it matter?" He realized he had spilled beer the other day on the shirt he now wore. He had hoped to have grabbed a different shirt in his dark apartment before leaving to come down here, but apparently, he failed in that regard.

"I didn't drag you down here so you can shake off a binge, Mr. Elder. I need your help. Desperately. I need you focused."

He waved her away, glancing around the lobby to take in as much as he could. The last thing he needed was some unknown woman criticizing his life choices. Cute as she was, he wasn't going to let her pull his strings in any way. "I assure you I can do my job just fine."

She lifted herself to his height, using her heels to gain a little bit of height on him, and locked gazes. "Are you sure?" Those eyes. Harvey turned away from her. "Who gave you my number?"

"Why is that important?" She moved to intercept his wandering eyes again, but this time he locked gazes with her and stared hard into her crystalline orbs. "I have money. You *obviously* need money. So how about we move forward, and I'll tell you why you're here?"

He gritted his teeth. He didn't like working for others—not in a professional sense. That was the beauty of private work. He could set the standards, for the most part. Work things out in his own timing. Yes, there was usually a time limit to things, but he could still find ways to work at his own pace. He felt like this was going to be a fast-paced case that she would want solved right away.

She caught his stare again. "Mr. Elder? Are you with me?"

He nodded.

"Good. Follow me." She turned from him and started through the lobby. He followed, scolding himself for setting a very bad first impression with this woman. She seemed nice, intelligent, and not hard on the eyes. But he reminded himself there were always sharks beneath calm waters. He couldn't be distracted by her, by his own thoughts.

He examined the lobby again, his eyes taking more in this time, his mind tracking the details.

The building itself was nice and warm, a welcome contrast from the raging sheets of rain outside. He would still rather be in bed, musing about how horrible life was. But this was the next best thing.

They passed the display case and he saw that the glowing flower was actually a tulip. Its petals glowed bright white. A silver placard was installed below the glass case that read: *The Twilight Tulip. Discovered 1997 by Augustine Rose.*

He listened to Jessica's heels clap against the marble tile and wondered how much money had been dropped into this place. The ceiling rose at least fifty feet and ended in glass sheets that gave a view to the pelting rain overhead. When they reached the receptionist desk, Harvey made it a point to grab one of the pamphlets off the counter. He opened it and found it to be an informative brochure on the botanical gardens, with a colorful map of the grounds.

Beyond the main building they were currently in stood the gardens themselves. The map indicated there was a gazebo, a hedge maze, a fountain—even what looked to be a mini forest. The rest of the pamphlet went into details about Augustine and the origins of the botanical gardens.

Augustine Rose founded the Midnight Botanical Gardens with the intent to preserve, study, and enhance the unique flora found in Midnight City. The Botanical Gardens is sustained completely by funds acquired by Augustine's unique research and contributions to the field of botany. She has received numerous awards in Plants and Gardens *magazine, has been featured on* Gardening Now *with Bobby Green, and has taught specialized classes on plant cross-breeding at Midnight City University.*

"I can give you a tour if you'd like," Jessica said.

Harvey folded up the brochure and shoved it into the pocket of his coat.

He continued to follow her toward the double doors he had

seen through the windows. Giant posters—made of what looked to be very thin canvas—hung on the walls flanking the double doors. Each one was of an artist's illustration of an exotic plant, with the plant's name in Latin written in a fancy font at the bottom.

The plants were none that he recognized. One looked to portray sparkling, somewhat iridescent vines. One plant had multi-colored petals. The one poster that really caught his eye was the one with blue-glowing grass on it.

"Those paintings cost ten grand each to make," Jessica said. "They are painted in a special chemical mixture that makes the paintings seem to glow and come alive."

He spotted something on the floor. He gazed down near his feet and saw an orange flower petal, charred black at the edges. The surface of the petal seemed to glisten under the lobby lights. He didn't want to touch it—maybe it could be evidence. Nor did he want Jessica to know that he had seen it. Not yet, until he knew what was going on. But he made a mental note of it.

"Mr. Elder?"

He looked up at her.

"I tell you that because you need to know how much money—and effort—has gone into this place. What you're about to learn about this place is that it's a money pit, but the reason for that is to bring beauty to Midnight City and to fund Augustine's research into the strange and beautiful plant life of this city."

That's nice, he thought. *Get to the point.*

Jessica paused at the double doors. Without the clacking of her heels, the room fell into deafening silence, letting Harvey hear the rain patter off the glass above them. It was a relaxing sound, but it felt like the calm before the storm. He already felt unwelcome, even though he had only interacted with Jessica.

He had no idea who stood beyond these doors or what problems would be dropped at his feet. A missing plant? There had to be more to it, and he was at a loss for information so far.

Jessica looked at him, her brow furrowed in distress. "Please don't allow how they treat you to determine if you'll help with this case. I'm sure the money is enough to keep you here, but if it's not, just know—for whatever it's worth—*I* need your help with this. Personally. And I know you don't know me, but I need you to trust that my whole reason for calling you in is for the sake of the plants here."

"Plants. Yeah."

She shook her head as she pulled on a lanyard that sat nestled in the waist of her black skirt. She held the attached keycard to a control panel on the right side of the door, but then waited a moment before pressing it fully against the card reader. "I grew up around plants, Mr. Elder. My mother was a botanist who received her degree months after my father died of cancer. *My* interest isn't so much in the science of the plants, but the plants themselves. They are living beings. Not on the same level as say, animals, or even you or me. But they are still living organisms, and I think they need to be treated as such. That's why I've invested so much of my time in caring for Gardens. That's why I will defend it." She glared at him. "At any cost."

Harvey took a step back, a bit surprised that Jessica's demeanor had suddenly escalated. At first, she had given off the impression she was somewhat docile, almost meek. But now she displayed an air of confidence he hadn't seen in many women—aside from Cynthia, or even Monique.

Jessica scanned the card, and the double doors unlocked. She pulled one open and motioned for Harvey to pass through.

He stepped into the next room. This part of the building

seemed to be a foyer of sorts—an entryway—to the gardens outside. The room was decorated in various potted plants of all different shapes and colors. A tall one stood directly to his left, purple limbs covered in spikes, with a top that came out to a pink-colored bulb. To his right, a tree rose up to just below the ceiling, its bark sparkling under the small garden lights that dangled from the ceiling. The pot didn't look as if it could hold the roots of this tree, making Harvey wonder if the tree itself was fake.

To his right sat a small bar nestled behind a marble countertop. Various bottles of liquor stood like sentries on a backlit wall behind the counter, varying shades of liquid courage glowing from the light. He found himself tempted to take a drink or two—at least calm his nerves—but he knew it would only dull his senses. He needed every ounce of wit he could muster to get through this.

Jessica motioned to the bar. "Augustine wanted there to be liquor stocked for the auction. Under normal circumstances, this is a tea bar—seeing as this is a botanical garden. I stashed all the tea materials under the bar counter though, so all that's out is the alcohol."

He said nothing to this. He hated tea, thought of it more as dirty water than anything that should be ingested out of pleasure.

Ahead of him stood more potted plants of varying forms. The plants all looked…alien…to him. These didn't look like any plants he had ever seen before, nor did they look or seem real.

Beyond the plants stood a doorless entryway that led out to the massive gardens outside. The Gardens were lit with small hanging lights that had been strung overhead, crisscrossing the air above their heads like telephone lines. They added a dim glow to the otherwise darkened area. The moon had not come up fully yet, and the dark sky above offered no source of light to illuminate the foliage around Harvey.

A purple-colored cobblestone path, line with stone benches, led straight from the foyer to a gazebo in the center of the area. A fire pit blazed underneath it, and couch cushions sat nestled around a fire. A stack of blankets sat piled on one of the cushions, no doubt there for the women in case it grew too cold. The wooden structure was otherwise occupied by a cluster of females in extravagant-looking gowns.

Jessica stepped directly in front of him again, filling his view with her perfectly-framed face. Her eyes pleaded. "You're about to meet Augustine. Please keep in mind her love is for plants. She doesn't deal with the outside world a whole lot. Please be patient with her."

The stomping of angry heels echoed through the hallway to his left. He turned and saw an older woman in a lab coat charging through the corridor, her blonde hair flowing behind her like a battle flag. When she reached Harvey and Jessica, her rageful gaze settled directly on the woman.

"You disobeyed a direct order! I specifically told you not to call in outside help. This is an internal case that I told you I would handle myself."

Jessica looked at Harvey and then smirked at Augustine. "You put me in charge of the Gardens. That makes me responsible for what goes on here. Including the theft of priceless plants. Harvey isn't part of any organization. He's a private investigator who will use the upmost discretion in solving our issue." She motioned to him, her thin arms acting like the twigs of a live tree. "Isn't that right, Mr. Elder?"

Harvey knew he couldn't play the offbeat drunk. Not with this other woman. It was clear she didn't want or think that they needed outside help. From her point of view, Harvey was an intruder in their little plant drama. But he wanted that fifty-thousand-dollars.

He reached out a hand. "My name is Harvey Elder."

The woman looked at his hand, then up at him. He saw the start of a sneer form on her face. "What do you know about plants, detective?"

He retracted his hand. He wasn't sure how to answer. "I know they die at my hand every time I try to care for one." He tried to laugh off the comment, but he could hear a groan seep out of Jessica's mouth.

"My name is Augustine Rose. I own the Gardens. I built them, with my own hands, so to say. I have discovered at least half the exotic plants you'll find around here. I don't tolerate those who disrespect what I do here. I've been known to kick customers out of the Gardens simply for acting belligerent or showing disinterest in my beautiful creations. If Jessica really wants you to help, you will do well to respect what I do here."

Harvey nodded. "I'm just here to help."

Augustine's lip twitched, and then turned into a full sneer. The crow's feet at the corners of her eyes became more pro-nounced, and she seemed to age ten years with the simple facial contortion. "We'll see."

Jessica turned toward him. "So, Mr. Elder, we—I—brought you here to help us solve the case of the missing plant. I—"

"It's more than that!" Augustine snapped, her face flushing red. "There's more at stake here than a missing plant. God, how could you be so frivolous with this matter?"

Jessica closed her eyes and took a deep breath. Harvey could feel the patience seeping out of the woman. "Rose, I am trying to handle this situation as best I know how. You wanted no police. No press. No interference. However, if nobody from the outside helps us, how can we get to the bottom of this objectively? You put me in charge of the Gardens, to care for its wellbeing. Let me do that."

Augustine took a step back and then inhaled a deep breath. "Alright, *child*. If you want to handle things, you can handle things." She turned to Harvey, her neck red with rage. "You won't get very far with them. They are in a realm so far above your…pay grade and character…you'll never get what you need from them. So good luck in your investigation, *detective*."

Harvey wasn't sure who or what she was referring to. He tried to say goodbye, but Augustine had already turned and was headed back down the hallway she had stormed in from.

"Forgive her," Jessica said. "She is passionate about what she does here. This place, the Gardens, is pretty much her creation. I have been assisting her with it since day one, but she can become obsessive." She motioned to the entry in front of them. "The Gardens are out this way. We have a retractable roof we move over them when it rains, or when the weather is otherwise tempestuous. There are cameras around the grounds, but Augustine contacted the security firm that monitors them and had them all turned off during the auction. Said it was to protect the anonymity of the bidders."

Harvey made a mental note of that.

"If you'll follow me, I'll take you outside to the crime scene and to your suspects."

Chapter 5

The gazebo stood decked out in strands of garden lights that hung under the roof of the wooden structure. A bonfire pit sat in the center of the gazebo, giving off enough warmth to make the area feel comfortable. Harvey could smell rain, though the ceiling above the Gardens was closed. It was an intoxicating smell, one that relaxed his nerves.

Or it *would* have relaxed his nerves, if he wasn't about to interview five different women about a missing plant.

"You're going to have your hands full with them," Jessica whispered.

She brought Harvey up the steps of the gazebo and paused, giving him a moment to take the scene into his brain. Five women, all dressed in different-colored gowns, and all wearing matching-colored half-masks decorated in ornate feathers and gemstones, much like what Harvey remembered seeing during the Mardi Gras in New Orleans.

What is this, a costume party?

"Oh, look." The woman wearing a forest-green dress stepped forward to the top of the steps. Even though he couldn't see her facial expression, something about the way she posed with chest out and her hands on her hips made Harvey feel as if she were talking down to him. "The storm did blow something in. A detective." She snickered and then took a seat on one of the couches.

"A detective?" A woman in a purple dress said, her voice oozing with disdain. She sat in one of the other couches, her legs crossed, the left one bouncing on her right. Harvey thought her purple heel would slip off her foot with the movement, but she played with the heel, dangling it from her toes while she smiled. "Who invited the fuzz to our gathering?"

"He's not with the police," Jessica said.

The woman in purple threw her head back, laughing. "Nobody cares if he's with the police, doll. The fact is, he's here to investigate us. To poke us, prod us. As if we are experiments to be abused through interrogation."

"My name is Harvey Elder. I'm here—"

An ebony-skinned woman dressed in a yellow gown had been standing by the fire. She turned to face him. "We don't care who you are, detective. We care why you're here. Augustine seems to think one of us is responsible for stealing the Death Rose. It's insulting."

"I still have to brief him on what's going on," Jessica added. "Ladies, it would benefit you to be honest with him when he questions you."

"Sure thing. And I'm buying the moon tomorrow," the woman in the green dress said.

Harvey took notice of a woman in a pink dress, sitting with her hands folded in her lap, staring listlessly at nothing. "What is her name?" he asked Jessica.

Jessica sighed. "They each have the name of a flower, to protect their identity. That one is Carnation. The purple, Lilac.

The green, Chrysanthemum. The yellow, Marigold. And the blue one over there," she pointed to a woman sipping on a glass of wine, staring into the fire, "that's Hydrangea."

"Great. Now I have to memorize flower names."

Jessica pulled Harvey down the gazebo steps and led him further along through the Gardens. "I never said this would be easy. Why do you think we're willing to pay you so much?"

"Valid point."

Jessica took him past clusters of tall trees that Harvey could barely make out in the shadows. They gave off some kind of energy...life. Harvey thought he heard chattering, as if the trees themselves were speaking in soft whispers to one another.

Ridiculous, he thought.

Jessica brought him to a grassy area lit with flaming tiki torches and Japanese paper lanterns hanging from strings above. A small koi pond gave the area a peaceful, exotic feel. Five white marble pedestals stood on one side of the pond, and on each of the pedestals rested glass domes, each with a different plant underneath.

Jessica put her hands on top of the glass dome with a red rose underneath. "This is why you're here."

"I thought you said I was called in for a stolen plant. That dome clearly has a plant under it."

"Could you withhold your annoyance until I've had a chance to explain the case to you?" Jessica used both hands to carefully lift the glass and set the dome in the grass at their feet. "This," she started, pointing to the rose standing upon the pedestal, "is the Death Rose. Well, it's a fake. A convincing fake."

Harvey examined the flower but could find nothing unusual about it. It looked like a normal red rose. "I don't understand."

"The women—they are here because Augustine put on a

masquerade auction to sell some of her rare plants. She plans to use the money to keep funding her research into more rare plants. It's an endless cycle with her, but that cycle has produced scores of valuable information on the strange foliage found throughout Midnight City."

"A masquerade auction? So, you guys weren't putting on a crazy costume party?"

Jessica stared at him. "Are you done? Of course it wasn't a costume party. Plants are serious business to Augustine, and she's been known to throw some strange marketing ideas out there to try to raise money. But this auction—the figures show she is going to pull in millions and millions of dollars, if we can find out what happened to the real Death Rose."

Harvey reached out to grab the flower, but Jessica quickly slapped his hand away. "Don't touch! Even though it's a fake, Augustine wants it to remain here until we find out what happened."

Harvey retracted his hand like a wounded animal. "What *did* happen? I still only have what you've been drip feeding me. Augustine threw a costume auction, sold a bunch of her pretty plants, and someone, somehow, managed to steal the real rose and replace it with a convincing fake. Right?"

"I found the fake after the auction was over. I was prepping the plants to go with their rightful auction winners. But then I noticed this…" She pointed to the petals of the Death Rose.

Harvey leaned in close to see what she was pointing at, but it just looked like regular flower petals. "I don't get it."

"The Death Rose is a normal rose with a lot of ancient superstition surrounding it. Texts say that once someone possesses the rose and hands it off to someone they truly love, then the rose will kill the recipient. No evidence of the crime."

Harvey chuckled. "Look, I've heard of some strange stuff in Midnight City, but c'mon. A rose that can kill someone? And if there's no evidence, how does anyone know it was the rose?"

Jessica nodded. "That's why I said there are a lot of ancient superstitions surrounding it. There have been two recorded cases of the Death Rose killing someone. But like you said, who really knows. Right? I'm with you on that one. I have my doubts. But still, the rose auctioned for close to eight-million-dollars.

"Now, look closely," she said as she pointed to the petals again.

Harvey leaned in even closer this time, noticing that the petal was a crimson color. "I see nothing but a red petal."

"Exactly," she whispered, her eyes meeting his. Those blue orbs stared back at him through the thick-framed glasses, and he imagined what it would be like to date someone normal.

He stood up and took a step back from the rose, shaking himself of that thought. He had to not fall for the wiles of a stranger. Innocent or guilty. He reminded himself that Jessica and Augustine were just as much suspects as the other five women.

"What's wrong?" Jessica asked, the worry lines in her face becoming more pronounced.

"Nothing. Are red rose petals unusual?" His tone came out somewhat sarcastic.

"Yes. In this case, anyway. The Death Rose's petals are dark red, with a black shine. That's the only way I could tell that this was a fake."

She pointed to another dome, this one with nothing underneath it.

"Someone steal that plant too?"

She shook her head. "Invisible Vines."

"You're kidding me."

"I am not."

He stared in at the dome, and from a certain angle with the available light, was able to see the iridescent curves of the vines spiraling up beneath the glass. "Interesting."

"Really? You find *this* interesting?"

'No' was his first instinctual reply, but he couldn't tell her no. Instead, he stood up straight and shrugged. "I don't know much about plants."

She waved him off as she set the glass dome over the rose. "I supposed you're used to murders and rapes and all sorts of sordid things."

"Sure." He glanced at the other plants under their glass domes. "What are the rest of these?"

She smiled and approached a dome with a white, glowing flower underneath. "This is the Twilight Tulip. One of the first flowers Augustine found on this land. It glows at night, goes black and loses its petals during the day."

"I saw one in the lobby as well. There are multiples of these flowers?"

"The one in the lobby is fake. Made of plastic and cloth. But to answer your question, yes, there are clones of some of these plants. That's part of what Augustine's research accomplishes.

"The Twilight Tulip is actually the source of many of the plants here in the gardens. Augustine found, many years ago, that the oil from the petals of the tulip had special botanical properties. When applied to other plants, she discovered the oil brings out amazing, almost magical, traits."

Harvey said nothing to this, just made a mental note about the tulip and the oil, in case the information became relevant later in his case. He wasn't sure he was buying all of this, but he had seen weirder things in Midnight City.

Jessica pointed to an orange-colored flower under another

dome. "This is the Bewitching Poppy. When worn, the poppy will mess with the recipient's mind, cause them to lose control of themselves. It's a pleasant, trance-like feeling, but you wake up not knowing what you did or where you went. I've heard you can be…controlled…through that. Very disturbing, if I'm to be honest."

Jessica smiled at Harvey, but he couldn't read through it. Was she smiling because she was happy, up to something, or being snarky?

"How could anyone see these plants and not have their view of the world changed?" she asked, staring down at the poppy. "To think that these are all part of creation, some of them just enhanced with help from *other* plants. It makes you wonder, what else is out there for us? These plants reside in Midnight City, but what if there are other, more stunning plants out there somewhere? It's exciting to think about."

"I guess."

She frowned. "I wouldn't expect you to understand."

"Why? Because I'm a detective?"

"Because you're a man. No personal offense, but the men I have come across don't appreciate things like this. I see these flowers and I see potential. Hidden potential. Like treasure that was buried throughout the world. And we're the ones who find the treasure and share our discoveries with the rest of the world. Men—usually—see things as merely objects. Tools. If it has no function, then it cannot be quantified as having value. Its purpose is what signifies its value. But something does not need to provide a service or a function in order to have value." Jessica touched the dome of a flower that had multi-colored, glowing petals. "Things can simply have beauty, have the mark of a Creator, and that gives them value."

Harvey had sincerely never thought about things like that. Yes, he was a man. And he did look at things as having purpose or being able to be used. But could something exist merely to provide beauty. To provide something else of value?

"Did any other plants go missing?"

She shook her head, her eyes filled with mist.

"I'll need to interview those costumed divas."

She wiped her eyes with the sleeves of her sweater. "I know. I honestly don't know how much you'll get out of them."

"I also need the records from the auction. Who won what flower, how much the bids were for, etcetera, etcetera, etcetera."

Jessica shook her head, her black bangs swaying like the branches of a willow tree. She sniffled and then answered, "I can't give you that information. If Augustine found out I revealed that to you, she'd fire me on the spot. Besides, I don't have it. It's all locked up in the administration office."

"Then how do you expect me to help you?"

She shrugged. "I don't know, to be honest. I don't even know why I brought you here. I feel maybe this whole thing was a mistake. You're going to hit a roadblock with the women. I promise you that. But, in the off chance you don't…If you can garner enough information to move things further, I'll be able to help you more. I have to know that you can take this all the way before I *really* stick my neck out for this."

Harvey sighed, glancing at the domed plants again. He could see why some people found these things so interesting. They seemed to defy the laws of nature. Even he couldn't deny that he was slightly fascinated by this.

Jessica drew close to him, her blue eyes looking up into his. "I'm sorry I dragged you into this. I really do think you can solve this case. I just…I think you're going to have a time of it. I'll help you as much as I can without putting my own career at risk. Beyond that, we'll have to see what your investigation turns up."

He felt a strange inclination to want to pull her in his arms and tell her that everything was going to be okay. But that would be inappropriate for a variety of different reasons.

Harvey wondered, briefly, what Cynthia would think of him solving a case like this. It was certainly a step up from running around Midnight City looking for old peoples' jewelry. But would solving this case prove to her he could do what needed to be done to pull his life back together?

He suddenly craved a beer and a bag of Doritos. He hadn't eaten a complete meal in a while, and he could feel the mid night hunger seeping in. He would have to eat later though. His instinct told him those five women weren't going to stick around very long. If he was going to treat them as suspects, he would have to question them now.

"Let the games begin," he mumbled to himself.

Jessica nodded and started toward the gazebo to call the women back into the foyer.

Chapter 6

H arvey looked around at the five women before him. Various colors of gowns, masquerade masks that covered the top half of their faces, and dispositions that screamed elite. He knew he would have his work cut out for him, but something told him this was going to be a long night. Or morning. He glanced down at his watch and saw that it was 2:21a.m.

Morning, he reminded himself.

"Alright, detective, what is it you require of us?" the woman named Lilac said. "As if you could require anything from ones such as us."

That got a giggle from the other women. All but the one in blue. Hydrangea, Jessica had said her name was. She sipped from the long-stemmed wine glass in her hand. Harvey noticed she wore blue lipstick.

Harvey pulled his small notebook from his coat pocket and set it on the marble counter of the bar. He flipped it open to the first blank page he could find—about eleven pages in—and then pulled out his pen. "What are your names? Your *real* names."

Lilac laughed. "That's rich. No, it's not. Because you're not."

Chrysanthemum stepped toward Harvey. "Why on earth would we give you our names. You realize this was a masquerade auction? The key word there is masquerade. We value our anonymity, so why do you think we'd just throw that away because you came waltzing in here like Dick Tracy?"

"I need to know your identities in order—"

Hydrangea set her wineglass on the counter. "I know what we should do!"

Lilac waved Hydrangea away. "Sit down, liquor fiend. Go back to drowning your sorrows."

Hydrangea laughed. "I have no sorrows. I just like wine. Is that a crime? Anyway, I have an idea on how to help our detective friend here. Since he wants our identities, let's give them to him." She strolled past Harvey and exited the double doors that led back out to the lobby.

Harvey stood, staring at the remaining women. The woman in pink—Carnation—was swaying, as if a violent breeze was pushing against her, back and forth. She didn't seem well. She stumbled forward and grabbed the counter for support.

Harvey reached out to take her hand and steady her, but she quickly pushed him away. "I'm good, detective. *Don't* touch me."

He put his arms up in a surrendering gesture. "Sorry. Just trying to help."

"You want to help?" Marigold said, pointing her finger at him. "Then turn around and leave this place. Go home. You aren't welcome here. This is business for the ladies. For those of us who have worked hard to climb the ranks we now occupy. Go back to your street stalking and binge drinking, and let us handle our own business, as Augustine wanted." She shoved her finger into his chest. Her long, pointed yellow nail dug its way into the front of his ribcage. "*Nobody* wants you here. You don't belong here. Get the hint."

The double doors opened, and Hydrangea entered the foyer, her hands full of various items. She set the small pile on the counter. Immediately, the other women darted forward to take possession of the items.

Hydrangea jumped in front of them, waving her arms in the air. "Stop! Stop."

Chrysanthemum, Lilac, and Marigold halted just short of the counter. Carnation dove behind the bar and vomited into the trash can.

Hydrangea turned to Harvey. "I have a game we can play with Detective Ding Dong over here. I took one item from each of our purses out there in the lobby. Just one item. No IDs. He has to use these items to guess who each of us are."

"Who gave you permission to go into my purse?" Chrysanthemum snapped.

Harvey could feel the anger in her voice. This hadn't been an idea of his, but he was glad it had been one of their own to present it. There was no way they would have accepted this way of doing things if it had come from him.

Hydrangea held up a single finger. "Hold on. Just listen. He's a detective, right? If he can't guess who we are by the items sitting here, he shouldn't even be a detective. Right? Am I right?"

Chrysanthemum approached the counter, examined the items, and then turned to Harvey. "Have fun." She left the foyer.

Carnation fell to the floor, her head in the trash can. Harvey knelt down to help her up, but she pushed him away, her mask still attached to her face, vomit dripping out of her mouth. "Leave me alone, detective!"

He stepped out from behind the counter, tired of getting yelled at.

Marigold stared at the pile of items on the counter. Harvey realized that if one of the women took an item from the pile, it would indicate their connection to that item. It might not be enough information for him to connect all of the dots...but it might be something.

Genius.

Marigold stormed off into the Gardens. Lilac did the same.

Hydrangea turned to Harvey and motioned to the pile. "All yours, detective. Have fun with that. I have to use the lady's room." She left down the hall opposite the one Augustine had stormed down earlier, toward what Harvey assumed were the restrooms.

Jessica stood, staring at the pile. "What kind of stupid—"

"It's brilliant," Harvey said as he grabbed the items off the counter.

"Brilliant? They're goading you. Mocking you, even."

"I know."

Jessica adjusted her glasses. "And that doesn't bother you, Mr. Elder?"

Harvey made his way back through the double doors and into the lobby area. He made a quick, mental note that the stray poppy petal from earlier was gone. *Someone must have retrieved it.*

He took a seat on one of the ornate couches, flipped on the small lamp on the round, glass end table, and then set the items on the small oak coffee table in front of him.

Jessica passed through the double doors, her heel clacks echoing through the large room as she made her way to the couch opposite him and sat down. "What do you hope to glean from a pile of junk taken from some rich women's purses?"

He felt his phone buzz in his pocket, and he withdrew it. Another message from the Midnight City Police Department.

Scene searched. Item of note: crushed poppy petals found in tracks of victim's shoes. More details to follow...

Harvey stared at the message for a long minute before Jessica finally pulled him back to reality.

"Mr. Elder? I asked, what do you hope to glean from a pile of junk taken from some purses?"

He slid the phone back into his pocket, the dreaded gravity of this case mixing with the excitement that it also brought. The murder on the other side of town could very well be connected to his plant theft case here at the Gardens. He wished he had picked up that petal earlier. He would have to keep his eyes open for more.

Harvey spread the purse contents across the table in a line. First, a book: *Phytotoxicology*. Then, a postcard from Wine Country. Third, a bottle of antihistamines. Fourth, a letter. And fifth, a sonogram.

He set his notebook out at the end of the line.

"This just looks like junk," Jessica said. "Especially that!" She pointed to the antihistamine bottle.

"I know. They *think* it's just junk. But I can use all of this to figure out their identities. Sooner or later." He picked up the small book. "What is Phytotoxicology?"

Jessica tapped her temple and closed her eyes. "It's the study of poisoning by plants."

He opened the book and flipped through the pages. There were countless chapters and sections on various plants and their poisonous effects on humans and animals. He skipped to a bookmarked page.

Deadly Nightshade / Atropa belladonna
This deadly plant is popular in many fictional stories, but do not take for granted that this is a very deadly flower with very real consequences.

Nightshade poisoning can cause dilated pupils, blurred vision, hallucinations, confusion, loss of balance, and a variety of other maladies.

Nightshade is said to have been used for many different things, even as anesthesia—when combined with opium. It is incredibly dangerous to children.

The antidote for nightshade poisoning is anticholinesterase.

"Nightshade," Jessica said, taking a seat next to Harvey.

He felt he should put distance between himself and her, but he didn't want to seem rude, so he just stayed where he was and handed the book to her. "Yes. I don't know much about the plant."

She took the book and skimmed the page. "Augustine is somewhat obsessed with it. She's always trying to concoct various plant varieties that have been crossed with the Atropa belladonna. She hasn't really been successful yet. I'm glad, because it can be a dangerous plant. Especially around children." She flipped through the rest of the book, and then stopped when she got to the beginning. "Hey, look!" She handed the book back to Harvey.

On the inside of the front cover was a bookplate with the name 'Tina Redfield.'

"Tina Redfield. Our first name." He scribbled the name in his notebook. "Tina is fascinated with poisonous plants, particularly the Deadly Nightshade."

Jessica curled a few strands of her hair around her finger. "Doesn't seem like much."

Harvey smiled, knowing it spoke volumes for a detective.

He set the book down and picked up the postcard. The

front said 'Wine Country' and had a photo of a vineyard on it. The back had an Italian stamp, and a message:

Winter,

I FINALLY got to see some of the most beautiful wine country for myself! What a dream. No wonder you suggested I take this trip. I also had a bit of the 'grape juice' to sample. Well, a lot of samples. You would be proud. LOL! I really wish you were here, sis! Maybe next time?

Lorie (hugs!)

The postcard was addressed to a W. Jackson.

"A postcard?"

Harvey set the item on the table, then wrote the name 'Winter Jackson' in his notebook.

He picked up the sonogram.

"That's someone's baby," Jessica whispered. "So, someone out there is pregnant?"

Harvey said nothing, just studied the sonogram. The name, Cerena Hatcher, was up in the top left. The image was dated October 20, 2021. He flipped it over and saw that the name 'Poppy' was sketched in what looked to be white corrective liquid.

He set the sonogram on the table and picked up the bottle of antihistamines. "Auburn Simpson, according to the prescription label."

"They have to be pretty strong to be prescription," Jessica said. "You can purchase over-the-counter antihistamines at any drugstore."

He shook the bottle. It was still at least half full. He twisted off the cap and slid a pill out into his palm. "They *look* like antihistamines."

Jessica nodded.

Harvey realized she was only inches from his face. He

dropped the pill back in the bottle and twisted the cap back on before placing the bottle on the table.

"One more," he said as he picked up the letter. A paperclip affixed a photo of a man and a woman at a bar, having drinks with one another. The word 'Loser' was written in black marker across the photo.

Haylie,

I know it hurts, but you have to get over him. You moved because he cheated on you. And he's still with the girl he cheated on you with! You could have been Mrs. Stockard - instead of Ms. Wilds - but thankfully you dodged that bullet. So, stop trying to reload the gun. Move on with your life. You deserve only the best, and he isn't it. I caught them down on 5th again, having dinner with one another. Here's a photo, just to prove it to you.

MOVE ON!

Your friend,

Stephany

"One of them moved here recently." Harvey said. "And it looks like she wasn't always an elite but became one through her own means."

Jessica said nothing to this. She stared at the items on the table. "I still don't see how you can connect any dots with so few items."

Harvey set the letter on the table with the other items. "That's why you're not a detective."

She looked away from him. "With all due respect, you have no idea why I'm what or who I am."

The edge in her voice caught Harvey off guard. He thought to apologize, then decided not to say anything at all. He didn't owe her—or anyone here for that matter—an explanation. *He* was the detective. *He* was the one they brought in to solve this convoluted mystery.

"I'm going to head outside and start interviewing our suspects."

Jessica ran her bangs behind her right ear and nodded, seemingly ashamed of her short outburst toward him.

Chapter 7

The woman in the purple dress—Lilac—stared at Harvey, her hazel-colored eyes peering at him with hostility behind the ornate mask. Dirty blonde hair spilled out around her neck. "Detective, did you think I'd answer any of your questions seriously?"

The air had grown significantly colder as the early morning waned on. The moon was beginning to make its pass over the Gardens, the full white creeping up over the edge of the glass ceiling above them.

Harvey sat on the edge of the small wall made of thick stone pavers surrounding the bonfire in the center of the gazebo, his back facing the warming flames. Lilac sat on the cushioned couch, her legs crossed, dangling that heel in front of her like a wild carrot in front of a mule.

"Lilac, right?"

She grinned. "You can't keep us straight, can you? Hear that, ladies? Here's a detective who can't sort through colors and names."

Harvey scribbled down some nonsense in his little notebook—a doodle of a house with a smoking chimney. He could keep them straight, but if they thought of him as a buffoon, he might get further than they expect him to. Jessica was right. Getting through these women was going to be hard. He was going to try a different strategy. Act the fool. Catch them off guard.

"Now, you said you were here at the time of the auction, right?"

Lilac leaned forward. "Are you drawing pictures? Like a child?"

He shrugged and then looked up at her. "You said you were here at the time of the auction, right?"

"You have no warrant, no actual legal jurisdiction here. And unless you're prepared to call the police—which I know Augustine has forbidden—you won't be getting that which you desire: my identity, or the identity of the other women. We wear these masks because we don't want you to know who we are. We don't want each other to know who we are. We're just here to buy some plants and head on home."

"Which plant did you bid on?"

She tilted her head back again and laughed, again. That heel bounced around like a fish out of water. "You are the stupidest detective I have ever met. The stupidest. Why would I give you that information?"

"Just asking."

"Just asking?" She stopped bouncing her heel and uncrossed her legs. "Detective, don't you find all of this a grand waste of time? I certainly do. Do you know anything about the five of us? We don't know anything about each other except for the fact that we are all filthy rich."

Harvey listened as he glanced at her left foot. A faded tattoo resided just below her ankle: an ornate vine that wrapped around into a circle.

"We all came into these riches through various means," she continued, "most of which don't really matter. What matters is that we have a ton of money, and we don't want the world to know who we are. These flowers we've been bidding on are just more baubles to add to our treasuries. They just take a different form than priceless vases or expensive oil paintings."

She leaned back in the couch and started bouncing her heel again. "Do yourself a favor," she said as she pointed to him with her long, purple-painted fingernail, "and scoot on out of here. You're out of your league."

Lilac sneezed, and Harvey made a quick note of it. "You sick?"

She looked at him with a confused expression. "Allergies, detective. I'm allergic to roses. I don't usually sit in a botanical garden in the wee hours of the morning ingesting every flora known to humans. Life has more to offer than that, wouldn't you say?"

Harvey doodled some more in his notebook. Lilac thought she was a brick wall, but she had already given Harvey some of the information he had been wanting.

"Life is short. I married into money to make the road less daunting. Play the game smarter, not harder, right? That's really all you need to know about me. Now, on your way. Go find a cheating wife or solve a bank robbery or whatever it is that you do."

Chapter 8

"Oh, detective. You're a bit outnumbered here, don't you think?"

Harvey doodled in his notepad again. This time he drew two stick figures kissing—he and Cynthia. He immediately scribbled out the drawing, feeling stupid for even sketching it.

Chrysanthemum leaned forward from the couch, her eyes peering out from behind the green-feathered mask. "What are you drawing there? You an artist?"

Harvey looked up at her, a bit taken off guard from her casual talk. "No. Not a good one, anyway. Just juvenile drawings."

"What do you want from me?"

He set his pencil down on the notebook. "Answers."

"Answers? I can give you any answers you want. Doesn't mean they are the right ones."

"Did you notice anything unusual during the bidding?" He picked up the pencil and started sketching in his notebook again. This time he drew a crude-looking flower.

Chrysanthemum paused before finally answering, "No. Augustine had it set as a silent auction. We tied our bids to our bank accounts, that way nobody could back out at the end."

"And you bid on…"

She chuckled. "You already tried that question with Lilac

over there." She pointed to the woman standing at the outer edge of the gazebo, staring out at the dark gardens. "What answer did she give you? Oh, that's right. She didn't give you one. Just laughed in your face—like she laughs in everyone's face."

"Do you two know each other?"

Chrysanthemum shifted in the couch cushion, then leaned back in it. She crossed her thin arms over her chest and seemed to stare off into the distance. "None of us *know* each other. But there are certain traits some of these women have that seem...familiar...to me. I can't divulge that information to you, but I feel like I know these women. Some of them, anyway. Strange."

"How so?"

She turned to him, sat up, and then motioned to the entire gazebo. "This crowd contains some of Midnight City's most elite. I can tell not by how much money they all have, but also by their attitude toward things. Most of them bid on these plants not because of their love for plants, but because of their love for *things*.

"I have a different attitude toward these matters. My love for plants is superseded by nothing. Ever since I was a little girl, I have been enamored by plants, starting with my mother's garden. It had every flower you could possibly grow—even the dangerous ones. As I grew older, I learned that flowers and plants aren't just for beauty. Some can be deadly. Some can be healing. Plants have so many uses to those who take the time to learn and understand. Tools, they are, in the right hands.

"My latest study," Chrysanthemum said, her eyes lighting up, "has me completely and thoroughly bewitched. I'm fascinated with the Deadly Nightshade. Did you know that in some cultures and secret tribes, deadly nightshade is ingested so that the user can develop an immunity to it? In case they are ever poisoned with it?" She leaned back in the cushions again, seemingly disappointed. "I doubt you know anything about plants. You're out of place here. You're even more out of place among us. I don't necessarily mean that as an insult, but even you have to admit your…kind…is like a weed amongst the rest of us flowers."

He shook his head, trying to kick out the sting that insult had inflicted on him. He *didn't* belong here. But he didn't belong in a lot of places he found himself as a detective. This was no different. Even if Midnight's elite were involved.

"I mean, really, detective." Her beautiful green eyes seemed to glow behind her ornate mask. "Do you feel welcomed here?"

He let out a sigh and shrugged. "Should I? Does it matter? I rarely feel welcomed anywhere."

She nodded. "Very true, I suppose." She stared at him, hands in her lap. He took notice of a large diamond ring on her left hand.

He motioned towards her, reaching out his hand. "May I?"

She glanced down at her lap and then raised her eyebrows. "Excuse me?"

"Your ring. May I see your ring? That has got to be the biggest diamond ring I've ever seen."

She let out a quick, jolting laugh, then raised her hand up so he could see it, wiggling the fingers of the same hand. "Beautiful, isn't it?"

He remained with his hand outstretched.

"You want me to take it off? You're not going to run off with it, are you? This thing is worth thousands of dollars."

"I don't doubt it." He waved his hand toward himself, smiling as he did it.

She struggled a moment to pull the ring off, and then set it gracefully in his palm.

Harvey took notice of her finger—the absence of any kind

of tan line. He then proceeded to examine the ring. It was indeed a very expensive looking piece of jewelry. He had no doubt it was real, either.

"How long have you been married...Chrysanthemum?"

She narrowed her eyes at him, briefly, but then relaxed her shoulders. "Five years. A fantastic man. Very intelligent. And handsome. He teaches, you know. Teaches classes at the university."

Harvey continued to examine the ring. The cuts on the stone were flawless. "Teaches classes on what?"

He looked up in time to watch Chrysanthemum place her fingers on her chin. "I can't tell you that, detective." She reached toward him and took the ring from his hand, slipping it back onto her finger. She had to wrestle with it for a moment before she was able to get it back in its place. "I fear I may have told you too much already."

Harvey nodded. "Maybe. Maybe not."

"Your eyes, detective. They give you away. You light up anytime you're eating a clue. You really should work on your poker face."

He looked down at the doodle of the flower he sketched, realizing he had drawn a rose.

"I have given you whatever answers I have, detective." She waved him away. "It's time you move on to the next stem."

Chapter 9

The dark-skinned woman in the yellow dress stared at Harvey with narrowed eyes. Those eyes were a golden brown and reflected the firelight. "So, you believe one of us did it? Stole the Death Rose? That's rich. Actually, it's us who are rich. So why would anyone *steal* anything?"

Harvey sketched a little balloon in his notebook, floating into the air, away from the world and its troubles. Troubles like bills. Troubles like dead careers. Troubles like women.

"Are you even present among us, Mr. Detective?"

Harvey looked up from his notebook at the woman sitting in the couch across from him. "Yes. I'm sorry…Marigold, was it?"

She folded her arms. He noticed the elegant—and very expensive-looking—silver and rose-colored watch on her right wrist. "You know very well what my name is. What is this, a detective trick to piss me off and get me rambling?"

Harvey set his pencil down on the notebook in his lap. "Is there something valuable you'd like to tell me? Something I can actually use in this investigation? Or are you just going to play games?"

"Play games? You think I have nothing better to do than play games? Typical."

"Typical?"

"Of men."

"Not sure what me being a man has to do with any—"

"Of course you don't see it. You're deluded by your own failings, as most men are. You know nothing of elegance, of beauty, of grace. All men saunter around like apes, destroying all life around them while claiming to be knights-in-shining-armor. What a croc."

"You think it's fair to judge me as a person according to your experience with various men?"

Her eyes seemed to enflame at this. "Various? Men?" Her teeth snarled as she said it, and Harvey could swear he saw her nails extend another inch.

"That came out wrong."

"As most things do out of men's mouths. Men are pigs, detective. All men. We women are the fairer species. We are more dignified, more wholesome. More *loyal*. I'm sure a man like you probably has a whole trail behind him of broken relationships."

He sighed. "Not really a fair point."

"Isn't it though?

Harvey stared into the golden-brown eyes of the woman named Marigold and realized he could almost see the hurt steaming off her person. She had been wounded, inflicted with heartbreak, and was trying to make it through her life without fully healing that wound. He could relate, as he himself was constantly running around with a bleeding heart.

"You see something interesting, detective?" The comment was loaded with bitterness.

"I know what it's like to be hurt," he said at the risk of being ridiculed. "To be discarded. And I know what it's like to try to function after that."

"I doubt that. Most men aren't ever capable of processing

emotion."

"That was certainly a stereotypical comment."

"Was it? You haven't experienced what I've experienced, detective. You don't know what I've been through."

"Enlighten me."

She shrugged, crossing her arms. "Why? So you can use everything I say against me later?"

"Humor me, then. Why do you hate men so much? Your distaste for them seems to venture beyond modern feminism."

She bit her lower lip. "The one I'm married to, detective, is a rowdy philanderer. Ventures through Midnight City, looking for another piece of flesh to…I don't think it would be proper for me to go into detail about that with the likes of you. Needless to say, he married me, but he finds me boring? Too much? I don't know. Who knows what goes through his mind? I would rather not know, to be honest."

Harvey glanced at the watch on her wrist again. The price range on it had to be at least five thousand dollars. "Why did you marry him?" he asked, already knowing the answer.

"This world can't be trusted. The only person you can truly, utterly trust is yourself. So, measures have to be taken to make sure that you, as a person, are taken care of. I married for convenience. Nothing more.

"On that topic, are you married? Is there some poor, helpless damsel that you rescued with your innate chauvinism?"

Harvey shifted on the stone pavers. As much as he was tiring of Marigold's constant attacks on the male gender, he felt the greatest impact when she had to bring up his relationship status. He thought of Cynthia, wondered where she could be right now, what she was doing. He wondered too if she would even care that he had agreed to take such a stupid case. These women were by far some of the most obnoxious suspects he had come across in his career.

Marigold grinned the grin of a hunter after wounding its prey. "I've made you uncomfortable, haven't I?"

"My personal life is nothing of note."

She nodded, then stood to her feet. "You look and smell like the trash, detective. Do you believe whoever broke your heart had a right to do so? Or are your misgivings the *result* of a broken heart?"

Harvey stared down at his own two hands. They were full of lines and scars from his past. "I don't know anymore."

"Piece of advice. This isn't your arena, detective. I promise you that. You're in a realm of the rich and the powerful. I'm sure you're used to dealing with the lower levels of hell, like the Underground or the downtown alleys. Get out of the clouds, return to the sewers. You won't survive up here. The lack of oxygen will kill you."

She ventured out of the gazebo, her heels clacking across the wood planks as she went.

Harvey glanced around at the women gathered in the warmth of the gazebo and wondered if she was right.

Chapter 10

H arvey really wanted a cigarette. It wasn't in his usual nature to smoke cigarettes, but the stress of this particular case—and the way his suspects were treating him—was pushing him to want to do things he didn't usually do. Marigold had made a valid point that made him wonder: Was he out of his place here? He was used to dealing with the lower-level scum of Midnight City and hadn't ventured too far 'above the clouds,' so to say. He had met detectives who dealt with the elites, and they were a different breed than he was. They were conniving, malicious, strategic, and much cleverer than he.

Harvey was used to dealing with cheating husbands, prostitutes, and serial killers.

The woman sitting in front of him with her back to the fire sipped on a glass of wine. Harvey guessed this had to be her fourth glass, at least since he had arrived. This could make getting answers out of her easier or more difficult, depending on her nature.

"Ask your questions," she said. "I am fully loosened up to answer them."

"Did you notice anything unusual before or during the auction?"

She swirled her glass. "Do you like wine, detective? I looove it, not only because it tastes good, but because it is a direct benefit defived...derklived...derived—that's it!—from a plant, a vine, actually. Fascinating. And so many people enjoy this benefit—some more so than others. I will admit that I have taken to enjoying it a teeeeensy bit more than I should at times. Even now, I feel a little...tipsy.

"Even so, I can hold my own. Do you like a good Chardonnay? Pinto...Pinot Noir? What about Sauvignon Black...Blanc? I am a bit of a wine snob, I guess. But it comes with growing up in a family of drunkards. Wine, beer, hard liquor—all of it was always just strewn about the house in half-dranken...drunken?...glasses or empty bottles. I hated all of it when I was little, because of the way it changed those around me, like my mother and father. Turning them into beasts. Angry beasts. But then as I grew, I embraced that which ailed me and made it my own."

Harvey just stared at her, his notebook open, pencil at the ready. This woman was definitely the type of person he was used to dealing with: a drunkard.

She waved her free hand at him, her eyes sparkling. "Oh, don't look at me like that. I'm not an alcoholic. I enjoy wine—not brandy or whiskey or any other hard liquors. Wine is more...elegant! More like the flowers in this garden. I spoke with some of them earlier, you know? Yes, they speak to me. I am a bit of a plant whispererererrrrr."

"Did you notice anything strange during the auction?"

She waved her arms around. "What isn't strange around here? Talking plants. The supernatural. This place is practically humming with life. Can you feel it, all around you?"

He could. It was a strange feeling—like a stranger in the room with you, hiding in the corner, watching you from the background.

"No. What flower did you bid on?"

"The multi-colored one. The Maddening Marigold." She

took another long sip of her wine.

Harvey remembered seeing that flower under one of the domes. "And what is that one's superpower?"

Hydrangea snorted and then choked on her wine. She slapped her chest, coughing as she fought to compose herself. "Oh my. That's funny. Superpowers? This isn't a comic book, detective. This is real life. That's why all of us are here, because those plants possessssesss special qualities that we all want to own. The Marigold can cause someone to return—in their head, anyway—to a place in their past. It triggers—like a gun!—something in the brain, feeds off the memories and turns them into something that feels real. Faskinating!"

Something turned in Harvey's gut. He didn't fully believe the nonsense about these flowers at first. But now, seeing a group of Midnight's elite shelling out millions for them...something had to be true about the rumors he had heard.

But that meant the effects of these plants equated to the same effects—if not worse—of the drugs that had been made illegal throughout Midnight City. So why hadn't any restrictions come down on this place? Why hadn't any regulations been passed in the botany field regarding these?

Then he realized the answer to his question was sitting right in front of him. The elite. They used their money and power to make sure there were no controls applied to these plants.

"You look lost in thought," Hydrangea said before she took another sip of wine, emptying the glass.

"Just putting the pieces together."

She swallowed the liquor and then set her empty wine glass down on the armrest of the couch. "You think you are. These pieces, detective, aren't really meant to be put together. These plants—they are grown and experimented with and then sold to the highest bidder so more plants can be grown and experimented with and sold. It's a cycle. But it's not one you will ever have any control over. This is Mother Nature mixing with human experimentation. There is no sssstopping that."

Harvey drew a crude-looking tree in his notebook, then wrote the word 'dangerous' in its trunk.

Hydrangea stood to her feet, wobbled for a second, then gained her footing. She reached an elegant hand toward him. "C'mon, detective. You can come with me to get another drink."

Harvey shut his notebook and stood to his feet without grabbing her hand. "I'm good. I have one last person to interview."

"You think these are interviews?" She laughed. "A detective maybe, but not too bright. You're the prey, not the hunter. All of these women—they fool around with their food before they consume it. Like wild animals. I just drink and drink and drink, and it dulls that ache that one finds within themself when they've seen the animals consume each other a little too much."

"Thank you for your time…Hydrangea?"

She reached out her hand. "Winter."

He gently placed his palm in hers. Her skin was sweaty and warm. He shook her hand.

She held onto his palm for a long moment, her blue eyes staring into his with intensity. "If you need me, I'll be inside the foyer, getting some more to drink. I would like your company, detective. You seem…friendly. Smart. We'll see how smart."

She finally let go of his hand and wandered out of the gazebo.

Harvey glanced down at the empty wine glass she had left behind. Deep blue lip marks stained the lip of the glass. He made sure nobody was watching him before he picked up the stemware. Most of the women had left the gazebo and were wandering elsewhere—probably talking trash about him. He lifted the glass to his nose and took a deep, long whiff. All he could smell were grape notes.

He set the glass down where he had found it and moved on to the next—and hopefully last—suspect.

Chapter 11

H arvey found Carnation sitting on a stone bench alongside the path connecting the main building to the gazebo. As he took a seat next to her, she said nothing, did nothing. She seemed lost, and her eyes looked glazed over. As he watched her, Harvey noticed her chest was moving in a slightly rapid fashion, and he wondered if she was having trouble breathing.

There was a strange glittering dust at the neck of her dress, and remnants of it on the end of her chin, only visible by the firelight's ability to cast itself in nearly invisible things. It looked like glitter—the same glitter that had been visible on the flower petal he found when first arriving at the Gardens. He wondered if it was coincidence or part of the grand design of this drama he found himself in.

Harvey held his notebook on his lap and sketched out a drawing of a carnation. The way he drew the flower—from the top down—made the design look more like a circular maze than blooming flora.

He looked up at Carnation again, and her gaze met his. "You okay," he asked her.

She nodded.

"Could you tell me about the auction? At least what you remember?"

She nodded again, only this time with her eyes closed. "I arrived a bit before the auction. I like to wander the gardens whenever I have the time. Just...wander. There is no place like these gardens in all of Midnight City. Paradise...in the midst of this concrete jungle."

"There's definitely no place like it in Midnight City." He meant to be sardonic, but the tone of his remark seemed to fall on deaf ears.

Carnation said nothing to his comment. Her hands sat peacefully on her knees, as if this was the proper stance for a lady. Her arms were thin, and her skin was an ivory hue that meshed well with the pink of her gown. She looked almost like an alabaster statue, poised and proper.

"I love the poppy," she whispered. "Something so simple about it. It's not flashy, like the rose. Or pompous, like the tulip. It's perfect. So many of the other flowers try to show off, to put on a show. But the poppy stands in its own natural beauty. It doesn't need to scream or flash a banner to make one know of its presence."

Harvey set his pencil down. The warmth from the fire on his back with the contrasting—and growing—cold in the Gardens made him somewhat drowsy. It was nearly three in the morning now, and he was feeling the waning night taking its toll on his mind. "Do you remember anything strange about the auction?"

She nodded. "These women. There's something familiar about them."

Chrysanthemum said the same thing.

"Familiar? How so?"

Carnation took a deep, slow breath and leaned back in the cushions. Her eyes closed, and for a moment, Harvey wondered if she had fallen asleep.

"Do you have children, detective?"

The question itself caught him off guard. "No."

"Shame. If I were to ever have a daughter, I would name her Poppy."

"Poppy?" He remembered the sonogram.

She nodded, her eyes opening. They looked clearer, more focused on him this time. But he could see the glistening tears forming in the corners of her pupils. Her lips looked as if they were stuck in a permanent frown.

She has to be under the influence of something.

"I wonder, though, if I would want a child in a place as strange as Midnight City. This city is corrupt. Not everyone sees the dark underbelly that runs through Midnight City. But I do. I see it, and it used to make me fear."

"I can understand that," was all he chose to say. He wasn't certain where this conversation was going, but it seemed she had things she wanted to tell him.

"Not anymore though. I faced that fear, and I rose above the ranks. Rose almost to the top. Someday, maybe, I'll be at that pinnacle. For now...for now I will remain content with what I have, despite what I have lost..."

He saw her rub her stomach.

Harvey glanced around the gazebo. Only two of the women were still lingering in this area—Hydrangea and Lilac. Lilac stood, leaning against one of the gazebo's pillars. Hydrangea rested across the length of one of the couches, sleeping by the looks of it.

"What exactly is it you've lost," Harvey asked. There was something incredibly personal to her comment about loss, and he knew he had asked too much, even though he thought he might already know the answer.

Instead of snapping at him in a rage, he saw tears fill her

eyes. She sniffled, and then reached her hand up to her face, probably forgetting she had the mask on. When she felt the mask, she shook her head. "I've lost more than you could ever know." With that, she stood up and left the gazebo.

Harvey sat there, contemplating her words for a moment.

Chrysanthemum left her pillar and sat in the seat Carnation had previously occupied. "Strange, don't you think?"

"What's that?"

She motioned to the Gardens. "This. All of this. I found it strange myself when I was invited to this shindig. An auction for supernatural plants. Priced in the millions. And a masquerade, no less. Then one goes missing. Then a detective shows up. And I get the succinct feeling that all of us women know each other from somewhere, I just don't know where. Maybe we've met in the grocery story, maybe at the bank. Could even be at our local bar."

Harvey shut his notebook with the pencil in it and stood to his feet, stretching. He felt—and heard—his neck crack. "What are you getting at?"

Her eyes seemed sharp, focused. "I don't believe in coincidence, detective. And in your profession, neither should you."

"I don't."

She nodded. "Good. I don't like detectives. I don't like busybodies. But I have a feeling it's no coincidence you're here. Remember that, please. Solve this so we can all go to our respective homes. I for one have tired of this place."

She stood and wandered off, leaving him there in the gazebo with the sleeping Lilac.

The woman stirred but did not say anything to Harvey. He thought to question her more but realized he had probably gotten all he would out of these girls.

He pocketed his notebook and decided to find Jessica to

see if she could help him piece some of his findings together.

Chapter 12

arvey found Jessica in the foyer, sitting behind the bar. She sat alone, and she didn't have a drink with her. She was scrolling through her phone, but as Harvey drew close, she quickly turned it off and slid it into the back of her skirt.

"Mr. Elder."

He put his hands on the marble counter and took a deep breath.

Those blue orbs looked out at him behind their lens prisons. She dropped her hands into her lap and smiled. "Anything to report?"

Harvey grabbed a bottle from behind the counter and set it down between him and Jessica. It was a tall, emerald-green bottle with a bright liquid sloshing around inside.

"You going to drink that? Now?"

He smirked. "Does it look like I need more alcohol in my system?"

She shook her head, and her body moved so fluidly, he figured her to be much younger than she most likely actually was. "Sorry."

He returned the green bottle back to its place behind the counter. "I'm trying to piece things together here. You have five women, all of whom are filthy rich from the sound and look of it. All have hidden their identities. And some of them seem to find the others familiar."

"Familiar?" Jessica cupped her chin with her right hand, as if she were about to go deep in thought over something. "How would they know each other?"

"Good question." Harvey took a seat on one of the barstools. "Who invited them? Augustine?"

Jessica nodded. "Yes. Said she needed money for further research. She sent the invites out, and I was responsible for answering any questions they had about the auction."

"So, Augustine has to know who these women really are."

Jessica nodded again, only this time she looked away, focusing her gaze on the hallway that ran to the other side of the building. "She does. But she wouldn't share that information with me. Said it was confidential. To protect these…women."

Harvey wondered if they were part of some cartel or mob that ran through Midnight City. The only reason these women's identities would need to be protected was to make sure other nefarious types – or other noble types – didn't find out who they were.

Harvey felt his phone buzz. He turned from Jessica and pulled his phone from his coat pocket.

Victim has wedding ring. Still looking into getting proper identification. Too difficult to distinguish last name. More information to follow…

Wedding ring? So, he was married. Not much to go on.
Harvey put his phone away and then turned back to Jessica. "Something important?" she asked.

"Everything I do is important," he said, more as a joke.
She frowned, seemingly taking offense at what he said.
"Sorry, was just trying—"

She put her hand up. "Sorry. I don't mean to be intrusive. It's just, I want to get this thing wrapped up."

He nodded. "Yes, that's nice and all, but sometimes these things take time. Especially when we're dealing with five women who all mostly refuse to answer questions directly."

She nodded and then used her hands to slide her bangs back behind her ears.

"Hydrangea gave me her first name," he said. "If she was telling the truth, she identified herself as Winter."

Jessica locked eyes with him. "That name doesn't sound familiar."

"Another one seemed out of it. Like she was under the influence of something."

"The pink one? Carnation?"

Harvey nodded.

"Yeah, she seemed that way to me too. Was worse earlier. I couldn't even get her to say anything to me before the auction. In fact, I didn't see much of her before the auction began."

"She said she was wandering the Gardens, talking to the plants."

"That may have been true. They were allowed to wander a bit either here in the foyer or in the gardens while I prepped the plants for the auction."

"And you said the security cameras were turned off?"

She nodded. "Augustine's orders. Said it was to preserve the anonymity."

The clacking of heels echoed through the foyer. Harvey turned to find Chrysanthemum charging toward him, the short train of her green gown flowing behind her like liquid emerald.

She reached Harvey and grabbed hold of his arm. "Detective! We heard a scream from the Garden. It sounded like Hydrangea."

Harvey stood to his feet and pulled his arm out of her grip. "Did you try to find out if she's okay?"

Chrysanthemum smiled. "You're the law in this place right now, right? Isn't that *your* job?"

Harvey started toward the gardens, aware that Jessica had come up right behind him. As he passed through the open entryway, the Gardens no longer smelled like rain. Floral notes seemed to dance on the air, filling his sense of smell with hints of roses, carnations, and lilacs. There were other smells in there too, but he couldn't properly pinpoint them.

When he was with Cynthia, she would fill her home with the scent of aromatherapy oils, usually floral-based. The same ones he could identify now. His heart ached ever so slightly, his emotions swirling within him, reminding him that Cynthia was out there somewhere, anywhere he wasn't.

A shrill scream echoed throughout the gardens, ripping him from any nostalgic memories he was in the mood to pursue.

"Where is that coming from?" Harvey asked, immediately recognizing the scream as Winter's. With the open space of the gardens, he couldn't pinpoint where her voice had originated from.

Jessica pointed toward the eastern corner of the grounds. "Sounded like it came from the hedge maze."

He started in that direction, following the purple path away from the gazebo and the main building. Jessica rushed to his side while Chrysanthemum stood, arms crossed, in the Garden's entrance.

He and Jessica ventured forward, using the small lights along the path to illuminate their way. Jessica drew close to Harvey, constantly bumping her arm against his as they moved through the gardens.

They crossed a line of hedges and entered a pathway that led down a long, floral tunnel. Glowing flowers covered the iron framework that shaped the tunnel, lending a spooky glow to their path. The path cut through thick, green grass that seemed to whisper under Harvey's feet. Even he had to admit to himself that the glowing plants were something of a neat trick of nature.

"Augustine had me build this. We call it the Flora Tunnel. Those flowers up top are bioluminescent. They glow somewhat naturally. Of course, they've been enhanced by Augustine's research."

Jessica's heel caught in the spacing between two path stones, and she nearly fell. Harvey caught her in his hands, saving her from making a very disgraceful tumble.

He released his grip on her arms as she stood up straight, flattening out her skirt and readjusting her bangs.

"Thank you," she whispered.

He said nothing, just continued moving through the Flora Tunnel.

The nagging thought took up residence in his head: *Is she playing me?* What if she was the one who stole the Death Rose? Under normal circumstances, she would have been the obvious suspect—the assistant to the one who got the glory, money, and honor. Jessica was a background shadow, performing the day-to-day operations while most eyes fell on Augustine as the face of the Gardens.

Augustine had it all: money, power, fame, and all the resources she could need to perform her strange plant experiments. She had no motive to steal her own plant—or steal money from any one of the bidding women.

But Jessica did. She was second fiddle, servant to the queen bee.

Harvey had quickly dismissed Jessica as a suspect at the offset because she was the one who called him in and the one who was insistent on the crime being investigated.

Why would someone do that unless they really wanted the culprit to be caught?

To deflect suspicion, he reminded himself.

He gave himself about a foot of distance from the woman so no part of her was making contact with him. He didn't want to fall for her wiles—if she was the culprit. As a detective, he had to keep his mind free of distractions. And she was certainly a beautiful distraction.

They exited the tunnel and came to a large clearing full of plants. Harvey noticed they were the same plants in the front of the building—Venus flytraps—but on a smaller scale. These came to just a few inches taller than Harvey. But they too seemed to watch him, their jowls open, waiting for some unfortunate victim to fall prey to their trap. Small floodlamps buried in the lawn illuminated the beastly creations, casting surreal shadows on them.

Harvey realized he could hear nothing now—no screams, nothing. He wondered what he would do if he found Winter dead. That would rule out Jessica as a suspect—mostly. She was with him when the screams were heard. But that wouldn't rule her out as a possible accomplice.

Harvey's mind tried to put the few pieces he had together, but some wouldn't fit right, wouldn't click. Why would Augustine and Jessica host an auction only to steal their own plant and not get paid for it? Why would the other women steal the plant when they clearly had enough money to simply outbid each other for it? And why would anyone pay so much for these plants to begin with?

They're plants, Harvey told himself. *Exotic, interesting plants, but plants, nonetheless.* Millions of dollars to purchase something that could die the next day? Then again, that was assuming everyone had a black thumb like Harvey did. If he even breathed on a houseplant wrong, it wound up wilted and dead without pause.

They reached a thin, iron archway that said 'Hedge Maze' in—appropriately enough—hedges intertwined into the arch.

Harvey sighed. *A maze. Great.*

Jessica took his hand, startling him. "C'mon, I'll lead us through. I have this thing memorized."

He reluctantly allowed her to pull him into the labyrinth. He had no chance of successfully navigating the maze by himself, not in a timely manner anyway. Jessica pulled him along the winding, jagged path of green foliage, nearly jogging as she yanked his arm this way and that.

The scent of wet foliage filled his senses, and he could feel the cold chill of the air within the maze's corridors, as if they were walking through an unconventional refrigerator. It was refreshing but irritating at the same time. The colder it became, the more difficult Harvey found it to process his thoughts appropriately. Tiredness was starting to sweep over him, and that, combined with the cold, dulled his senses.

"I have the maze memorized by layout since I've been here in the Gardens since the beginning," Jessica said. "Just another right…and then a left…and then—" Jessica pulled him into a clearing in the center of the maze. He broke free from her grip and glanced around, hoping to find Winter. Instead, he found nothing save for four stone benches all organized in a square facing each other, and an ivory podium in the center of them.

"I don't get it," Jessica said. "I know this is where the scream came from. I'm sure of it."

Harvey couldn't argue with her point. He had heard the same scream, and he too could have sworn it came from this part of the

Gardens. He approached the podium and found a bronze plaque that seemed to have been installed to commemorate the Gardens.

This plaque commemorates the establishment of the Midnight Botanical Gardens. In 1999, Augustine Rose commissioned the Gardens to be built at the edge of Midnight City, upon land that is imbued with remarkable properties. The mysteries surrounding these lands cannot be fathomed, but Augustine has used this magic to both preserve and manufacture exotic flora that can be found nowhere else in the world.

There on the edge of the plaque sat a multi-colored marigold corsage. Harvey examined it to see if there was anything to it. It looked to be made of cloth, but other than that, nothing seemed out of the ordinary. "What is this?"

Jessica examined the flower. "One of their corsages."

"Corsages?"

Jessica looked dumbfounded, then guilty. "I didn't tell you about their corsages?"

Harvey took a deep breath and let it out slowly in an attempt to keep his cool.

Jessica took a step back and smiled nervously. "Augustine had corsages made. They're fake replicas of the flowers that were being bid on. Winter was wearing this one. The Maddening Marigold."

"These are replicas? Fake replicas?"

Jessica nodded. "I'm sure of it. They were each to wear one of the flowers they wanted most. It was to instill a little bit of competition. What's strange though is everyone picked a different flower, so the competition factor didn't go very far."

"Where is Winter?" she asked.

Harvey wondered the same. Where had the screaming woman run off to? He looked down at the marigold. The petals shimmered with glowing colors. "You're sure that was *her* scream?"

"Positive."

Harvey took another look around the clearing. None of the benches held anything of interest. Besides the corsage, the podium was empty save for the plaque commemorating the Gardens. There didn't seem to be any evidence of a tussle.

"Do you think she's around here somewhere?" Jessica asked. "Maybe in the maze?"

Harvey shook his head. "No. Let's head back to the foyer." He left the corsage there on the podium.

Chapter 13

J essica escorted him out of the hedge maze, past the fly-traps, through the Flora Tunnel, and back into the main garden. They followed the path back to the foyer, where they found Winter standing behind the bar, her blue gown contrasting the gold trappings of the room. She wore a thick, white coat made of vintage fur, and sipped on a tall glass of alcohol. Harvey had trouble discerning whether it was wine or hard liquor in her stemware.

"Where were you?" Jessica asked.

Winter finished another long sip and then set her wine glass down gingerly on the marble countertop. "I've been here, in the building," she said, her eyes twinkling. "I had to use the restroom—what with all the wine I've been drinking tonight. Then I came over here for another drink."

"We heard you scream," Jessica said, exasperation in her voice. "From the hedge maze."

Winter smiled. "Why would I scream? And why would I be in the hedge maze?" She tightened the front of her coat. "In the cold? In the dark?"

Harvey glanced down at Winter's wine glass. It was the same wineglass she had been using in the gazebo—her blue lip prints were identical in placement at the rim of the glass as they were when he interviewed her.

"Something catch your eye, detective?"

He locked gazes with her. "Winter, right?"

Her smile faded as quick as fog dispersing in sunlight. "You have a good memory."

"Wouldn't I have to? You're the only one to give me your name. If Winter really is your name."

She lifted her glass to her lips and took another sip as she shrugged her thin shoulders. "What reason would I have to lie about my name?"

Heels echoed across the tile, and Harvey turned to find Chrysanthemum and Lilac approaching from the gardens.

"Detective," Lilac said, smirking. "Looks like you've been busy chasing your tail."

Chrysanthemum pointed to Winter. "I see she's doing what she does best—drink Midnight City under the table."

Winter scoffed.

"Do you have something to tell me? Something I can actually use?" Harvey asked.

"In private," Lilac said, her eyes watching Winter.

"Can you excuse us?" Harvey said to Winter.

Winter took a last sip of wine and set the empty glass down on the countertop. "Of course. I'm going to go nap off some of this grape juice." She withdrew from the bar and marched—rather, stumbled—out toward the gazebo.

Lilac's gaze now fell on Jessica. "We said in private."

"I'm the one who called him here," Jessica snapped. "You really think you have the right to—"

Harvey took gentle hold of her arm. "Please," he whispered in her ear. "I need answers. I'll meet up with you after I speak with them."

She huffed, but then marched back through the double doors into the lobby.

As the doors shut behind her, he turned to Chrysanthemum and Lilac. "What is this about?"

Chapter 14

Lilac sat on the barstool, dangling her purple heel as she had done numerous times during his visit here to the Gardens. She giggled while she did it, and this only seemed to irritate Harvey even more.

"Did you ladies want to actually tell me something important, or is this more of the games you like to play? I have an actual investigation I'm trying to pursue."

Chrysanthemum crossed her arms over her chest and took a deep breath before releasing it. "Remember what I said earlier, detective? About how all of this was strange?"

He nodded. He had set his notebook down on the counter while he took a seat on one of the barstools. Next to him, Lilac smiled devilishly and acted almost as if she was trying to toss her shoe at him.

"Well, Lilac and I know each other."

"How?"

Chrysanthemum shook her head. "That's all I'm going to say for now. You just need to know that this auction—this whole setup tonight—wasn't a coincidence. I'm sure Augustine would love the money that comes from the sale of her precious plants, but there's been more to this since the beginning.

"I'm not a thief, detective."

Lilac slapped her hand down on the countertop. "Neither am I!"

Chrysanthemum placed her hand on Lilac's shoulder. "Easy." She turned to Harvey. "I really can't tell you more than that. We both know each other. That's enough for you for now. I trust you can put the rest of the pieces together."

He glanced down at his notebook. He had scribbled some notes about Winter and the hedge maze. "Did you two hear the scream earlier. From the hedge maze?"

Lilac smiled giddily.

Chrysanthemum stared at him, her green eyes full of answers she wasn't going to share with him. "Keep your wits about you. I'm sure you'll piece this together soon enough. I'm sorry we can't be of more help. Our interests in telling you this are simply to help you find the culprit. We aren't thieves. If I were you, I'd be investigating Carnation. She seems to have her head in the clouds."

Harvey realized he didn't know where Carnation was. He shut his notebook and looked across at Lilac.

The woman glanced down at her foot and then extended her leg toward him. The tip of her heel almost touched his knee. "I'm curious to see how far you get with all of this, detective. You seemed a little smart at the start, but you are now clearly in over your head."

"Well, I have the likes of you two giving me convoluted, cryptic answers to everything, so what do you expect?"

"I expect you to play the part of the detective. Not the victim. I wonder…" Lilac leaned forward, staring directly into Harvey's eyes. He wanted to break eye contact with her, but her piercing gaze pulled him in with their chaos. "You're lovestruck."

Harvey stood up from the stool. He had to find Jessica and

see if there was more information he could get regarding Augustine and the auction.

Lilac grinned, sharp teeth flashing white. "Lovestruck. And lovesick. You pine for someone, don't you? A woman who has unfortunately left you for better prospects."

Harvey stared at the floor, at his brown shoes.

Lilac stood and positioned herself in front of him, placing both hands on both of his shoulders. She stared at his forehead until he lifted his head and locked gazes with her. Being this close, he could smell her rose perfume. The scent wasn't strong, but he caught whiffs of it. It was enough to conjure memories of Cynthia.

"Detective, you are drowning in love. I see it in your eyes. It makes you...distracted. Fractured. As much as we like to toy with your kind, Chrysanthium – Chrysanthmeum—" she turned to her friend. "Why the hell couldn't you have picked a different flower to emulate?!"

Chrysanthemum said nothing.

Lilac turned her attention back to Harvey. "She and I want you to find the thief. If for no other reason than to clear us. We don't like unwarranted heat coming down on us. You may not understand the world of the elites, but you understand well enough when victims do not want to become the suspects. Clear your head. Forget the lost love."

Harvey noticed the small scar in the corner of her lip. The discoloration—the markedly white tint—made the small imperfection stand out just barely.

Lilac let go of his shoulders and stepped back. "My friend and I are going to head back out to the Garden. Please hurry. We have other business to attend to." With that, she started toward the open doorway.

Chrysanthemum nodded to him before she turned and

followed.

Chapter 15

H arvey found himself alone at the bar, looking over his notes while drinking a glass of water. The tasteless beverage did little to wake him up or give him something of substance to snack on, but it would have to do. He knew he had to seek out Jessica, but he needed a moment to think, to try to put the pieces together, to try to figure out just what was going on around here.

He knew now that at least some of the women knew each other. How? He didn't know. Maybe they lived in the same neighborhood? Maybe they were part of some elites' club? He knew the 'how' could be important, but he wasn't going to get those answers quite yet.

He knew Winter was more than just an auction bidder. She was playing a game with him—though he didn't know to what end. He knew she was the one who screamed from the Garden, but why lead him to the hedge maze? Was it so he could find the corsage? Maybe the corsages played an important role in all of this.

He kept turning in his mind the flower petal he first observed on the floor when he arrived here. It had been cleaned up by the time he returned to the lobby. But by who? And why?

Was it the same kind of petal found on the murder victim on the other side of Midnight City? Could that be an important clue he overlooked? The petal was similar to the Bewitching Poppy Jessica showed him in the gardens. Was all of it connected?

He scratched the stubble around his chin, wondering where Jessica fit in all of this. This beautiful woman who had been pulling him along through this whole investigation. She was holding cards to her chest—cards that could very well help him solve this investigation much quicker than he currently was.

The double doors of the lobby opened, and Jessica strolled in. From the strain on her face, Harvey could tell she was frustrated about something. She stormed over to him, glanced around the foyer and down the hallways—as if she was looking for someone or something—and then let out a low growl.

"Did you listen good from the other side of the door?" he asked.

Jessica put her hand to her chest, feigning offense.

"Yes, I know that's what you were doing during my chat with those two, because it's what I would have done."

Her eyebrows slanted downward, and she put her hands to her hips. "Glad to know you think so little of me."

He shrugged. "Just pointing out facts. So, is something wrong? You seem pretty worked up." He closed up his notebook and stuck it into his coat pocket. He didn't wish to leave it laying around. Though his doodles and sketches were probably nothing more than alien babbling to most everyone who would see them, he didn't want to risk anyone getting the wrong idea. Especially Jessica.

She balled her fists and fumed. "I called the security firm that watches our cameras. Augustine didn't actually shut them off, not completely. She told the firm to continue monitoring them, but not to let anyone know. She also told them not to allow me to access any information from them."

"Suspicious."

Jessica slapped her palms against the side of her legs. "I know one of the guys in the firm. I asked for him, and he said he could send me a printout of where everyone was at while I was prepping the flowers for the auction. I tried to explain to him that that information was useless, as I was with the flowers that whole time—so how would anyone have been able to do anything during that time without me knowing about it?"

Harvey shrugged. "Did he send you that information?"

She nodded. "I have to access it on my computer, in the administration office. But If I do that, Augustine will be alerted. She won't be happy, especially if you're with me."

Harvey stared down the hallway. "You hired me to solve this case. At every turn, I've been blocked or lied to. If there's information that we can get our hands on that will help turn this case around, we need to get it."

"I just don't know what to do. At this point, I believe Augustine might have something to do with all of this, but there's no way of telling for sure unless I break whatever confidence she has in me."

Harvey pulled his botanical map out of his pocket and lay it open across the marble countertop of the bar. He pointed to the administrative office that resided at the end of the hallway to their left. "Unless we want to explore the gardens again, then this is the last place we have to investigate." He then pointed to the laboratory on the other side of the map. "Unless you want to go directly to the source."

Jessica saw him point to it, and then threw her arms up in the air. "I can't. You have to understand, my loyalty to Augustine has been absolute. She took me on as an apprentice before she even found the plants that would lead to all of this. I wouldn't betray her by giving you access to things she wouldn't want you to see."

"Or *you* to see?"

Her eyes lit up. "What do you mean?"

"It's obvious there's more to this than even you know about. Stuff she's kept from you. What if some of that stuff came to light and you were blamed for it? Wouldn't you want to put a stop to that before something like that could happen?"

Jessica took a seat on the barstool and pondered this for a moment. "I could go in there myself and see what I can find. At least then she can't point the finger at me for allowing a stranger in there."

Harvey shook his head. "No. I need to go with you and see what's in there for myself. You might miss a detail or hint that I could use to piece this whole thing together."

Harvey's phone buzzed in his pocket. He pulled it out. Another text from his friend in the VFPD.

Victim identified as Victor Paxton. Still trying to find next-of-kin information. More information to follow...

Harvey stared at the message for a moment, then put his phone away.

"What is it?" Jessica asked.

He shook his head. "Nothing. Just a friend."

"At almost three in the morning?"

He shrugged. "A detective has many friends in many places at many different hours."

She raised an eyebrow at him. "I guess."

"Do you think I'm keeping something from you?"

She put her hands up. "I don't know. Does it matter? You're the detective. I'm just the lowly peon who is here to assist you."

"I never called you a peon. There are just certain pieces of information I keep close to my chest. May or may not become valuable at some point. I don't have time to tell people every little detail I'm cataloging in my head."

She sighed. "Fair enough. What do we do now?"

We?, Harvey thought. She did think of herself as his assistant. It made sense, seeing as she had been Augustine's assistant for so many years. Still, Harvey reminded himself to be wary.

Harvey stared down the hallway in the direction of the administrative office. He knew something had to be in there that would help his puzzle pieces connect better. Maybe the identity of these women? Maybe information on Augustine—even Jessica? Maybe there was something awry with the origins of the Gardens. Of course, they needed to get their hands on the security information, but he knew the bigger prize was the documents that may be hiding in that room.

Jessica sat on the barstool, but her body was still in motion, like a child that had just ingested a pound of pure sugar. She was abuzz, both with nervous energy and frantic determination to make the right decision. She clacked her acrylic nails across the marble counter. "She's been my friend, you know? She took me in when nobody else would believe in me."

"Maybe she had a reason for doing that." Harvey said the words, but quickly regretted it.

"Maybe. I guess nothing is out of the question at this point, huh?"

He nodded. "Look, I'm not really one to encourage you to

turn on your boss. But the sooner we get to the bottom of all of this, the better."

Jessica ran her hands through her long, black hair, and Harvey felt himself, for a split second, pining for her. There was an elegant chaos about her. She was sophisticated, intelligent. But she had layers, and he loved it when women had layers and weren't just wearing superficial masks.

Idiot.

He frowned, realizing he was simply trying to distract himself from the fact that Cynthia had rejected him. All of him. Women did indeed have layers—every woman—but until you knew what those layers were, you had to remain on guard. One of them could be the end of him.

Jessica turned to him, stood up from the stool, and nodded. "I'll get us into the admin office. But we have to be quick in there. It won't take long for Augustine to notice we've gone in there. Once she realizes it, she'll be even quicker to shut us down. I may even lose my job for this."

Harvey nodded. He would hate to see Jessica lose her job, but why would anyone want to work for a known criminal if Augustine was in fact guilty of any of this?

Jessica led him down the hallway, her heels clacking against the tile, noisy with purpose.

Before they ventured down the hallway, Harvey looked out at the gazebo. Lilac and Chrysanthemum were there, with Marigold. All three wore coats and were lounging in the couches, but it didn't look like they were interacting with each other much. Carnation was notably absent from the group. He realized Lilac and Chrysanthemum might have had a valid point, stating what they did about Carnation. The girl had been acting weird earlier in the investigation, and since his interrogation of her, he had seen nothing of her. He made a mental note to go looking for her once he and Jessica finished their exploration of the administrative office. If he went searching for her now, Jessica could easily change her mind and then he might never (easily) get into the office.

Jessica led him down the hallway to an office where a gold name plate with Jessica's name adorned the front of the door. She pressed a combination on the door's keypad that Harvey regrettably missed witnessing, and then opened the door to a mid-sized office.

A desk sat at the very end, while bookshelves lined both walls to their right and left. A lone lamp sat on the desk, bleeding soft light into the room, making it difficult for Harvey to see clearly what books sat on the shelves. He imagined books about plants and flowers, or anything to do with botany.

The room had a strange mixture of scents to it. He picked out rose, but there was also the smell of sandalwood—incense.

"Augustine and I use this as a library as well as an office," Jessica mentioned. She led Harvey to the desk. A computer sat quiet on the surface of the oak furniture. Two three-tiered filing cabinets stood next to one another behind the desk. A closet with a numbered keypad lock stood off to the side.

Jessica took a seat at the computer. "Don't touch anything. We have to be in and out. If we're quick enough, I can fabricate some stupid story about how you needed some paper to write on or something. The longer we take though, the more suspicious she'll become."

Harvey cared for none of what she said. Instead, he watched as Jessica typed in her password into the computer and then used the mouse to journey around the desktop, searching for the email icon. When she found it, she clicked on the little envelope and waited for the email server to come up.

While she did that, Harvey examined the filing cabinets. They were like treasure chests to an investigator. Who knew what information resided within them that could help him wrap this case up in the next half hour? Then he could go back home, to his dumpy apartment, and get some sleep. Wake up late. Lounge the rest of the day away. Maybe partake in a beer or two. Or three.

He had to get inside one—preferably both—of the filing cabinets.

Jessica quickly turned to him and waved her hand to shoo him away. "Don't touch those. Those are Augustine's."

"Why are they in here?"

"We share this office. It has my name on it, but she uses it as well when she wants some quiet time to think or read."

"So, the books?"

"All hers."

Harvey wandered over to one of the shelves. They were made of oak and would have cost a fortune to line both of the wall of this office in them. They were the types of shelves Harvey had seen in millionaire's studies or the offices of multi-billion-dollar CEOs, but not something he would expect to find in the library of a botanist.

He scanned the shelf, noticing that almost every single book was tucked neatly in its place, flush against the back of the bookcase. Except for one. He walked the length of the shelf and tugged on the lone volume.

It was a book titled: *Stitions of Super* by Paran Meitzer. He recalled hearing of that name before—Paran.

"Find anything you'd like to sit and read, detective? I'm still waiting for the stupid security firm to send me that file. They had better hurry, or all of this will have been for nothing."

"Paran Meitzer. I've heard that name before."

"Everyone in Midnight City has. Don't you remember, Mr. Elder? He was that crazed librarian who took his own life and the life of his wife and kid a couple years ago."

Harvey's memory spun into recollection, and he suddenly remembered that particular case. He hadn't been assigned to it, but his partner at the time had been. Harvey, meanwhile, had been on a suspension.

"Wasn't Paran diagnosed insane years before that?"

Jessica groaned. "I don't remember. Wouldn't you know more about that, seeing as you're the detective? All I remember is that he claimed that voices from the Void told him that he and his family were in danger, and that the only way to protect them was to take their lives with his. He believed there was an eternal realm for those with the courage to kill those they loved. He was a sick, sick man. I get ill just thinking about it."

Harvey flipped through the book. "Stitions of Super? Creative title, I guess."

"That's a volume of superstitions he wrote about. Most of them originate in Midnight City. He was even hellbent on making the public believe that aliens had at one time visited our city. What a clown."

Harvey fell on a dogeared page.

The Death Rose.

Many legends surround the existence of the Death Rose, however, there has never been any concrete evidence that can prove these myths to be real. The Death Rose was discovered in the 90s by Augustine Rose, however, the plant's origins date further back through various transcripts and ancient texts that tell of its suspicious nature.

It is said that the Death Rose — if given to another with romantic interest on the heart — will grant death to its recipient. There have been documented cases in the past detailing the death toll following this foreboding flower, however, nothing but superstition has been able to tie the deaths to the rose itself.

No part of the flower is toxic, nor does the plant exude toxic gases/pheromones. The flower is said to have originated at the bottom of an Aztec sacrificial pit, dating this plant at least hundreds of years old.

"Got it!" Jessica shouted.

Harvey put the book back on the shelf and made his way to the computer. He saw a surveillance map on the screen with certain places marked with a glowing green 'X' on them.

"The report they sent is just a snapshot of where everyone was at shortly before the auction. What a waste—wait a minute. Look here." She pointed to the computer monitor at an 'X' that was in the Admin Office.

"Is that you?"

"No. The snapshot is timestamped at 11:28pm. I was in the gardens, prepping the last of the plants. I know for a fact that Lilac and Chrysanthemum were in the gardens with me. Augustine is the mark here, in the laboratory. That's where she spends most of her time. Marigold was here, in the lobby with Winter, drinking wine. That leaves…"

"Carnation."

"What would Carnation be doing in here?"

Harvey shrugged. The girl was becoming more and more a study of strangeness as the night and morning rolled on. "Was she in your computer?"

Jessica's fingers danced along the keyboard as she pulled up various screens. "No. Nobody has been in it since I was last on it, before the auction."

Harvey turned and scanned the room.

"There's nothing here but files. And the cabinets are untouched."

Harvey eyed the closet door. "What's in there?"

"Not much. Just a small safe Augustine built in there. Maybe some coats. I don't really know. I stay out of it. It's got a coded lock on it that I don't have the combination to."

Harvey approached the code panel. It had a keypad that looked a lot like the ones that used to be on payphones back in the day.

He took out his fingerprint powder and performed a dusting of the keypad. He watched as black fingerprints materialized on three of the numbered buttons.

"Oh, wow, Augustine is not going to be happy about this."

Harvey rolled the numbers around in his head. "If she wants to find out what happened to her flower, she'll just have to deal with it."

Jessica drew close to him. He could still smell the hints of cherry blossom perfume lingering on her sweater. "Well," she said, her breath warm when she spoke, "technically it was me who called you in. Yes, I do believe she wants to find out where the Death Rose went, but to be honest, I think she's more concerned with keeping her elitist bidders happy so she can procure another event like this in the future. She's more about money and the science behind all of this than the practicality and beauty. Those things are more…my department…I guess."

"Nine, seven, and one. Do those numbers mean anything to you?"

"I feel like they should. Augustine programmed this door panel. Maybe she used her birthday? Those numbers don't match that though."

Harvey remembered seeing the Twilight Tulip display at the front of the Botanical Gardens when he first arrived. The date the flower was first discovered—1997. He punched the number into the door panel and a thick lock disengaged from within.

"Very clever," Jessica said, her voice a slightly higher pitch than it had been all night. Harvey could sense the nervousness in her voice. He had no doubt that Augustine knew they were in here now, but why she hadn't come to stop them was a mystery to him. One of the many mysteries he seemed to be facing at the moment.

Harvey pulled the door open. Inside the small lit space was a bench attached to the back wall. A large floor safe had been installed off to the side, on the floor. The safe seemed to be locked still. But on the bench was a red rose, laying on its side.

Jessica lifted the flower into her hands. "This is the Death Rose." She turned it over in her hands, careful with the thorns on the stem. "From what I can tell, it's the *real* death rose. How did this get in here?"

Harvey noticed a scattering of poppy petals around the bench, all charred at the edges, like the ones he found earlier, and possibly the one found with the murder victim on the other side of the city.

"We need to get this to Augustine's lab," Jessica said as she headed out of the closet.

Harvey grabbed her arm as gently as he could without letting her leave. "Hold on."

She turned to him, Death Rose in hand, looking a bit miffed that he had taken hold of her.

He released his grip and put his hands up in surrender. "Hold on."

"Why? We found the real Death Rose. Security showed that

Carnation was in here, so she must be the one responsible. We return the flower to Augustine and then you can wrap up this case. I hired you to find the Death Rose, so you've done that. Augustine can still get her bid amounts from the women out there, then kick them out. Carnation can be arrested. It's settled."

He looked at the petals on the bench. "It doesn't make sense."

"This makes perfect sense," Jessica said as she adjusted her glasses. A few stray bangs escaped the confines of her mane and danced around freely, drunk and alive. "Carnation stole the rose, stuck it here in the closet hoping nobody would find it."

Harvey shook his head. "No. Why would she steal it and then hide it in the closet of the person she was stealing it from?"

Jessica shrugged. "I don't know. Maybe we're dealing with a really stupid thief?"

"None of the women out there are stupid. Maybe material-istic, and some of them seem to be drugged or drunk. But not stupid. Carnation in particular doesn't seem stupid. She seems under the influence of something."

Jessica set the Death Rose on the surface of the desk. She clasped her hands together in front of her and let out a long, irritated breath. "What are you thinking happened?"

Harvey stared at the petals on the bench some more, his mind trying to piece things together. "I don't know. But we need to find out more about those women out there. Their ac-tual identities. I think I've figured out their names—their real names—from those items Winter pulled from everyone's purs-es earlier. But I still know nothing about each of the individual women." He stepped out of the closet and immediately moved toward the filing cabinets. "Especially Carnation."

Jessica darted in front of him, holding her arms out as if she hoped to stop a charging bull with her delicate frame.

"What are you doing? You can't go in these."

Harvey pulled his lockpick kit from the inside pocket of his coat. "I have to. If you want to find out what's really going on around here, I need to see what's in these cabinets."

Jessica shook her head. "No. I can't let you. Augustine will have my head if she were to find out I let you break into her cabinets."

He chuckled, unrolling the kit in his left palm as he moved around her and approached the lock with a thin, worn pick. "She's already going to have your head for letting me in here."

"Okay, fair enough. But I can explain this away, especially if I show her we found the Death Rose and explain that it was Carnation who stole it. I can't explain you breaking into her filing cabinets."

"Well," Harvey said as he heard the small click of the lock disengaging on the first cabinet, "you better prep a good excuse then." He pulled the top drawer open.

Chapter 16

The contents of the filing cabinet did little to interest Harvey. Paperwork, paperwork, and more paperwork, all regarding the botanical garden's financials, the funding of the research Augustine did, and the figures of what various donors had given to the Gardens over the years. Lots of numbers, and Harvey didn't do well with numbers. Not when it came to this, anyway.

He held the property deed to the Gardens in his hand and turned from the cabinet to hand it to Jessica.

She sat at the desk, her hair a mess, her eyes tired, her glasses set on a stack of the financial records that Harvey had already emptied from the cabinet. She took the deed and set it down in front of her. "What is this?"

Harvey shrugged. "Looks like the deed to the Gardens."

"Why is this important?"

Harvey turned back to the filing cabinet.

Jessica put her glasses on and examined the document, then went to throw it off to the side when she did a double take. "Hold on."

Harvey turned from the cabinet again and moved until he was behind her, peering over her shoulder. "Did you see something of interest?"

She pointed to the signatures at the bottom of the deed. The assistant to the mayor of Midnight City, Felicia Brubaker, and Augustine's signatures were there, with a date stamp of February 24, 1997.

"So what?"

Jessica put her glasses back on and pointed at the signatures again. "You must be losing your touch, Mr. Elder. Don't you see what I see?"

He looked at the names: Felicia Brubaker and Augustine...Paxton.

"I thought her last name was Rose."

"It is," Jessica said with a smile. "Now. Paxton must be her maiden name? But that doesn't make sense. She's been Rose ever since I've been her assistant, which has been quite a while."

Harvey slipped his phone out of his pocket and reviewed the last text message he had received from his friend in the police department. The name of the victim on the other side of the city was Victor Paxton.

It couldn't be coincidence. The petals. The murder victim. Carnation. Augustine. Was Victor Augustine's husband? Had to be.

Harvey slid his phone back into his pocket and stared down at the property deed. He still felt he was missing a piece to this puzzle. But what?

He turned back to the filing cabinet and continued to dig around through the files, what few were left. More financials.

Jessica continued to muse over the property deed. "I don't know what you're really looking for in there," she said. "We've gone through both cabinets, and there's little to nothing—"

"Found it," he said as he reached down into the bottom drawer of the second cabinet and pulled out a manila folder that was stamped 'Confidential' on the front. He set it on the surface of the desk in front of Jessica.

She groaned. "What is this?"

"I don't know." He flipped the folder open to sheets of paper with photos attached. "Looks like someone was doing research."

"Could these be the women at the auction?"

Harvey flipped through the papers, reading the notes someone—most likely Augustine—had taken on the various people whose photos were paperclipped to the top of each of the pages.

Cerena Hatcher
Age 34

Cerena excelled at the top of her classes in business and graduated some years ago with a multitude of honors. Having a stillborn child messed her up in the head though, and she quit business and settled down with a man only a few years her senior. She used to work hard for what she has—now she just takes off everyone else's plate and manages to survive as an elite that way. I've tried to discuss things with her, but she blows me off as if I don't have anything valuable to say. She's in the prime of her life and seems to think she knows it all. I'm hoping someone will show her otherwise, because this spoiled brat doesn't seem to appreciate the benefits those in our circle already have. I don't believe she will ever be grateful for what she presently has.

Tina Redfield
Age 48

Tina has managed to keep herself single for many years now. After the untimely death of her husband (he fell off a skyrise, I believe), Tina has managed to do well for herself, running a successful chain of herbalist shops throughout Midnight City and surrounding cities.

This one has a healthy obsession with plants—particularly the poisonous kind. Her research on the nightshade family is unmatched by anyone within our circle. She is incredibly intelligent and, most of all, perceptive. This makes her a decent threat to those of us who would like to keep our positions. I will have to keep a very close eye on this one.

Auburn Simpson
Age 27

The youngest member, this one married into wealth but has learned to handle it fairly well. Her beau is a man very high in the ranks of Midnight's elite, owning multiple businesses and having rumored links to the criminal underground. She doesn't love him though, and it shows. She is constantly flirting and romancing other men, especially ones that can further her own goals.

This girl took a beating when she was younger. A junior high bully clocked her in the lip, giving her a very subtle scar. She's tough as nails. Auburn has an obsession with death and an allergy to roses, which helps explain her fangirl passion over the Twilight Tulip. Definitely one to look to for promotion at some point. I believe she would handle it well...with the right mentor.

Winter Jackson
Age 56

Winter does well for herself owning her own vineyard. That would normally impress me if I didn't already own three of my own. However, I must

admit that Winter's single vineyard does almost as well as my three com-
bined, so she knows her wine. And from what I've seen, she certainly
knows how to ingest and enjoy it.

She has a lot of potential, and she is a good candidate, even though she is
fairly new to all of this. She will prove to be as cunning as some of the others.
The ironic thing is, she has a sister in law-enforcement. I've actually
attempted to retrieve more information on this sister of hers, but she seems to
be a ghost. This does make me wary of Winter's affiliation with our group.
Is she here on her own volition, or could she possibly be working with her
sister? Only time will tell, I suppose. I must keep a very close eye on her.

Haylie Wilds
Age 32

I don't know what constructive things to say about Haylie. Haylie is still
young, somewhat inexperienced at life, and has a hard time letting go of
anything that pertains to her emotions. She is a ticking time-bomb of feel-
ings, but if she could learn to control them, she might be able to move
forward in life.

She was cheated on by her ex, and then she moved to Midnight City to
escape her heartbreak. This is at least something I can sympathize with. I
am hoping Haylie will one day become a strong, independent female who
will rise to the top, but only time will tell. I've made it a point to steer her
away from a relationship at the moment so she can (hopefully) focus on
what really matters.

Harvey read the profiles and let the information soak into
his brain. Jessica perused the document but said nothing about

the women.

"What's going through that brain of yours, Mr. Elder?"

"You can call me Harvey."

She raised her eyebrows at him. "You don't like formalities?"

He put his hand up and closed his eyes. "I just don't like being called Mr. Elder. Just call me Harvey."

Jessica put her hands up in a mocking gesture. "Okay. Harvey."

He looked down at the folder full of notes on the five women. He felt he knew who was who now. But he still felt like there was a piece missing.

He jumped out of his seat and opened the closet door again. He pointed to the flower petals on the bench. "What are those?"

Jessica peered around him. "Petals."

"Yes. What kind?"

Jessica scooted past him into the closet to get a closer look. She examined the petals, careful not to get her hands on them too much. It seemed she too was somewhat wary of what they could be or what they could have on them. "Looks like...poppy."

"Poppy petals?"

She nodded, backing out of the closet. "Yes. The Bewitching Poppy. I'm not sure what those are doing here though."

"I saw one in the lobby earlier."

"The only Bewitching Poppy was in the gardens."

"The only one you *know* of."

She stared blankly at him.

"All I'm saying is, there are probably things you don't know, especially regarding your employer and your place of work."

Jessica looked down at the manila folder. "You know who these women are?"

"Yes." He grabbed a scrap of paper from the desk and jotted down the names of the women and their floral counterparts.

He handed the sheet to Jessica. "I need you to indicate who wore what corsage."

She took the paper and began recording the information he requested.

It was then that Henry noticed a book sitting in the right corner of the desk. It lay flat on its front, with the back cover facing them. He reached over Jessica—drawing dangerously close to her beautiful face—and picked up the book.

"This yours?" he asked.

She glanced up quickly at it, shook her head, then went back to writing out the corsage types for each of the women.

He flipped the book to the front cover. The title read: *Ancient Cults of Midnight City* by Peter Valhal.

"Cults, huh?"

Jessica glanced up at the book. This time, her gaze remained on the cover. "You found that here, on the desk?"

He nodded as he opened the book.

"Strange. I didn't think Augustine was into that sort of stuff."

"Cults?"

Jessica nodded. She finished her note and slid the paper to the edge of the desk in front of Harvey. "She is superstitious to a degree. She has to be, I guess, to run a place with such remarkable plants. But she's not really into group settings, such as cults. She's more of a lone wolf. I mean, I've even tried to get her to go to lunch with me and she complains about how she has too much work to do, or that there's too many people 'out there.' I couldn't imagine for a second that she would participate in anything remotely close to a cult."

Harvey flipped through the pages of the book, scanning the pages for information regarding various cult groups to have been recorded in Midnight City at one point or another.

Cult of Dolphins—The name is deceptive, as the Cult of Dolphins has nothing to do with dolphins, persay, but actually with the communication traits of humans and animals in general. Members of this cult believe animals can 'talk' to humans—and vice versa—through an ancient universal language that did in fact originate with dolphins. Though this might seem like a worthless trait, some fringe outliers believe this language can be used to speak to cryptids that are believed to reside within hidden places of Midnight City. The language is called the Messtic Tongue, and it has already been used to speak, quite successfully, to bears, dogs, and even penguins. This universal language cannot be spoken by just any human, but only people with a distinctive gene known as the EI chromosome.

Harvey flipped through more pages, shaking his head. *The things people will believe nowadays.*

Stones of Esther—This cult worships a massive stone rock that contains a cluster of various precious stones, all which are said to have originated within the singular piece of rock. Studies have been done on the rock, and it was found to have originated in space. It is theorized to have broken off from a massive asteroid that passed closed to Earth's atmosphere some years ago. Members of this cult believe the stones—which include ruby, emerald, and diamond—are said to hold mystic alien powers. Member are required to touch the stones and then put themselves in harm's way to prove the protective power of the gems. It is believed that roughly 35% of those performing this initiation right survive. Tests of the protective nature of the gems are rumored to include standing in front of moving trains, leaping off bridges, and self-inflicted gunshots.

Harvey scratched his head at how stupid people could be. "You have to be a real dolt to believe half this stuff."

Jessica lifted her head from the desk. Apparently, she had dozed off while he was reading the book.

Harvey was about to put the book back in its rightful place on the desk when he noticed a thin cloth bookmark dangling out the back of the volume. He flipped to the page that was marked. A logo was depicted at the top right corner of the page—two hands opened up, with a rose in the midst of them. A circle of vines came around the outside of the hands.

Order of the Vine—A secret society of botany-enthusiasts who use their wealth and free-time to procure and preserve rare and exotic flora. It is unknown who actually runs the Order. The existence of the Order is known because of rumors that leak out from the Order itself from time to time. It is said that each member is required to prove their love—and dedication—to botany by ingesting their choice of a poisonous—and often deadly—plant in order to be inducted into the society. Most members choose the deadly nightshade, which can cause hallucinations, paralyzation, and loss of balance. Some do not survive this process, and this is believed to be responsible for some of the disappearances of wealthy elites within Midnight City. The Order is believed to be responsible for the theft/acquisition of over two dozen rare flowers from within the boundaries of Midnight City over the last decade. Where these plants are being held—and who oversees them—is unknown.

Jessica stood up from the desk and stretched. "Anything interesting in there?"

Harvey showed her the page on the Order of the Vine. She took the book, yawning, and then examined the entry. "Yes," she said once she finished reading it. "I've heard of them. Augustine actually mentions them from time to time. She hates the Order, thinks they've been responsible for stealing some of the plants she has been trying to get her hands on."

"So they exist?"

Jessica shrugged. "I believe so. Augustine believes so. I've never met anyone in the Order though. I don't believe—to the best of my knowledge—that anyone from the Order has ever stolen anything from the Gardens."

Harvey allowed this new information to settle in his brain, to work its way in between all of the other fragments he had been trying to piece together.

He took the sheet of paper Jessica had filled out off the edge of the desk and examined the names, adding the real names of the women next to the flora names Jessica had indicated.

Carnation / Bewitching Poppy	Cerena Hatcher
Chrysanthemum / Invisible Vines	Tina Redfield
Lilac / Twilight Tulip	Auburn Simpson
Hydrangea / Death Rose	Winter Jackson
Marigold / Madding Marigold	Haylie Wilds

Jessica glanced over his shoulder. "I don't know how you managed to connect all of the women with their identities, but how does that help us?"

"Hydrangea, or rather Winter, was easy. Her liquored state matches her love for vineyards. Carnation, or rather Cerena, lost her baby. Miscarriage. Lilac, or rather Auburn, has a scar on her lip, and she has an allergy to roses. Marigold, or rather Haylie, was cheated on by her ex. The photograph. And Chrysanthemum, or rather Tina, has an obsession for plants, particularly the poisonous kind. Hers was the book on Phytotoxicology."

Jessica stared at him. "Impressive."

He shrugged. "Simple deductive work." He folded up the

sheet of paper and shoved it into the pocket of his coat. "We have to find Carnation...Cerena Hatcher...right now." Harvey started toward the door.

Jessica grabbed the Death Rose and scrambled to catch up to him. "Why? What's Carnation—rather, Cerena—have anything to do with this?"

He exited into the hallway and stormed toward the foyer.

Chapter 17

arvey and Jessica returned to the foyer. Harvey half-expected to find Augustine marching down the hallway toward them, but the hallway and foyer were suspiciously empty.

"I'm surprised Winter isn't here, drinking all the liquor." Jessica set the Death Rose on the marble counter and then peered behind the bar. "Most of our stock is still here. I guess she does have *some* self-control."

Harvey peered out the open doorway into the gardens. He looked out toward where the gazebo was and saw nothing but darkness. The fires had been put out. The little lights illuminating the pathways were off. Nothing lit the gardens.

Jessica drew to his side. "Why is it so dark out there?"

Harvey's phone buzzed. He slid it out of his pocket and glanced down to a headshot of an older gentleman with gray hair and a gray, neatly-trimmed beard.

This is the murder victim. Seems to be all the information we're going to get tonight. Still don't know his cause of death. He's married, name is Victor Paxton, and he had the poppy petals in his shoes. Will talk to you tomorrow.

He slid the phone back into his pocket, fully aware Jessica was eyeing him, most likely hoping he would share something with her.

Not yet, he told himself.

The cold air whipped through the foyer, carried on a breeze that swept through the gardens. Harvey glanced up at the garden ceiling and noticed that the glass roof had been retracted, leaving the gardens open to any rain that might want to pour down on the plants. The sky still looked cloudy and dark, but there didn't seem to be any precipitation at the moment.

Jessica pulled the front of her cardigan together tight. "Something isn't right."

Harvey pulled his sidearm from the holster under his arm. "I know. Stay here."

She grabbed his arm before he could enter the gardens. "Stay here? Wherever you go, I'm going with. We have no idea what's out there. I think we should head to the lab and just talk to Augustine. Maybe she sent the women home."

Harvey holstered his weapon. "You're right." He followed Jessica as she led him to the laboratory at the end of the hallway opposite from the side the admin office was on.

A coded entryway locked them out of the lab. Jessica input her code into the reader, but it beeped and flashed red.

Harvey pounded his fist on the door. "Augustine? I need to speak with you. Open up, please."

Nothing.

Jessica tried the code again, but it gave the same defeating beep and red light as before. "I don't understand it. It's the same code I used before the auction. Did Augustine change it in the time we've been out here?"

Harvey rattled the door handle, but realized he wasn't going to get very far going this way. He wondered if whatever he needed was most likely in the gardens.

He turned from the door and stormed down the hallway.

When he reached the foyer, he burst through the double doors to the lobby, but found nobody there either. He peered out the windows to the parking lot outside and saw everyone's cars still parked in the same spaces they were in when he first arrived here.

He made his way back to the foyer. Jessica paced back and forth in front of the doorway to the gardens. The tapping of her heels had no rhythm, no pattern, just chaotic pitter patter against the marble tile.

Harvey pulled his gun out and headed out into the gardens. When Jessica tried to follow, he gently nudged her backwards, back into the foyer. "No. Stay here. I'll be back."

"What do you expect me to do while you're out there exploring the darkness?"

"I don't care. I'll be back." Harvey's eyes fixated on the gazebo. It wasn't likely all five women would vanish like this, unless they wanted to leave. But their vehicles were still here. It also wasn't a coincidence that something like this would happen in the twenty minutes he and Jessica were breaking into Augustine's office files.

"Just wait a sec," Jessica said as she entered the lobby through the double doors. She returned a minute later with a small flashlight, handing it to Harvey. "Just be careful."

He nodded. "Thanks." He turned the light on and held it close to the gun as he pointed both out toward the gardens, shining the light out onto the gazebo. He could see the couches and the put-out fire pit. The smell of spent firewood and extinguished flames wafted in the air, adding a cozy ambience to the rainswept night.

"I think maybe it's time we involved the police. Don't you?"

Harvey's gut told him she was right. This had escalated beyond what he had been brought in to handle. Instead of just interrogating a few rich snobs, he suddenly found himself in the midst of something he couldn't explain. Missing women. Missing flowers. Maybe even a cult. And he was pretty sure a conspiracy of some sort was afoot.

He stepped into the gardens, his flashlight beam strafing across the colorful foliage, bringing it to life in the dark.

A loud cranking noise roared from behind him. He swung around in time to see retractable doors slide in place over the open doorway and seal him within the gardens. Jessica pounded on the glass windows before rushing down the hallway, presumably to find a way to reopen the doors.

Unless she was the one to shut them.

He cursed under his breath, but somehow wasn't at all surprised. The gardens were now a trap, and he had stepped right into it. Now it was time to find out who the hunter was.

Chapter 18

H arvey took a deep breath of the cold air, inhaled the smokey scent mixed with floral patterns. He hadn't wanted to believe Jessica could be in on this whole thing, but he couldn't be sure. Not yet. There were too many clues, too many wrong paths and dead ends in this investigation so far. He wasn't sure who he could trust. Jessica had indeed called him out here to investigate. Augustine acted against it. And the five women who had been toying with him all night were most likely *still* playing games with him.

Harvey knew the only way out of this now was through. Sure, he still had his phone and could call the police. But what good would that do? By the time they showed up, the characters in this play would have scattered like roaches under sunlight. It would do no good in help if he hoped to solve the mystery.

If someone wanted him dead, this was the way to find out who.

He started down the purple-stoned path, reaching the gazebo. He cautiously made his way up the steps. The cushioned couches were all empty, save for the pile of blankets the women had been using earlier. Smoke and embers flitted up from the fire pit. He could still feel the warmth that was fading from the pit.

He decided to venture further into the gardens. There was something in here that someone wanted him to see, and he knew he wouldn't get out until he saw it. Whatever *it* was. He wondered if they wanted him dead. What if Augustine was so angry with him snooping around her precious Gardens that she wanted him taken out—permanently? What if Jessica wanted him offed? If so, she played a good game. Most likely, it was one of the other women who wanted him dead—if anyone wanted him dead.

He started toward the other end of the gazebo to explore further into the gardens, but his flashlight beam flashed on something sticking out from between the blankets. Harvey approached the couch, his nerves rattling away like a tin shed in a tornado.

He pulled back the top layer of blankets and stumbled backwards when he saw the blue gown and the pale face.

Winter's body lay there, lifeless, her body placed on the couch in such a way that her arms were at her sides and her legs stretched out to the end of the cushions. She wore a black trench coat to keep from the cold.

He slid his gun in its holster, knelt down, and felt her pulse. *Dead.*

He gently removed her mask and set it to the side. She had vomit leaking from the corner of her mouth. He examined her neck, her arms, and her legs, but found no other sign of foul play. There on the armrest of the couch stood a half empty glass of wine. It looked discolored under the flashlight beam. Harvey bent over and took a whiff, smelling something like animal urine reeking from the glass.

Harvey knew little to nothing about plants in general, but he knew when someone had been poisoned.

His phone suddenly rang, and he slid it out of his pocket, hoping to answer it before it could alert someone to his presence here at the gazebo.

"Yes," he whispered.

"Mr. Eld—Harvey," Jessica started, "I can't open this door. I've tried, but the panel seems to be busted."

"It's fine. I'm going to look at a few things out here. Just try to get it open or find me another way inside the building."

"Okay. There's another door that leads to the laboratory, from the other side of the Gardens. But it's coded, like the one on this side."

"I'll cross that bridge when I get to it," he said.

"Be careful." Her voice was meek, soft, and it made his heart ache a bit.

He disconnected the call and slid his phone back into his pocket.

He patted Winter's dress and jacket in the hopes of finding a clue or something—anything—that could help him find out why she had to die. He found nothing.

He shined the light around the gazebo, checking the couches, the fire pit, the wooden flooring. He spotted something on the floor, something like a wrapper. He bent down and lifted a small, folded piece of note paper. The position of it was underneath one of Winter's now-dangling arms.

She must have had this in her hand when she died. Whoever killed her must not have seen it.

Harvey glanced around, making sure nobody was within his vicinity before he unfolded the note and read what Winter had written as her last words in this life.

Detective,

You're closer than you think you are, but there is much more going on than you know. The theft of the Death Rose isn't just about money or even the plant itself. There are other forces at work here. You must know, I am not with them. By them, I mean The Order of the Vine. Please, stop them. I left something for you in the hedge maze.

Winter

Harvey folded the note and shoved it into his coat pocket. He stood underneath the gazebo, staring down at Winter's body. Was she referring to what he had already found in the hedge maze, or had she put something else there, after he left last? He knew it was time to call the Midnight City PD, but if he did that—if he spooked whoever was responsible for this—he would never solve this case, and Winter's killer would go free.

Harvey took Winter's arms and placed them straight at her side. Then he took the blankets and gently placed them over her body. He would have to lead police here once they were called in.

"I'm sorry," he whispered.

Harvey pulled his pistol and stepped out from under the gazebo, making his way with the flashlight toward the hedge maze he and Jessica had explored earlier. Finding his way back to the maze was easy enough. Finding his way *through* the maze proved difficult this time. Harvey liked to pride himself on his memory, but the cacophony of events over the last few hours had proven to create a jumble of facts and observations in his mind that he was still having a hard time sorting through.

A light fog had settled through the maze, a combination of moisture from the rain and the changing temperature throughout the gardens. He stumbled through the labyrinth, his company merely the noise of his boots on scratchy lawn as he tried to follow the route he remembered Jessica taking him through earlier.

He wound up at the entrance of the maze.

He cursed. He closed his eyes, trying to remember the route again.

He opened his eyes and navigated the maze again.

He wound up at a dead end.

He managed to backtrack to the entrance of the maze again.

He stopped and simply listened to his surroundings. Not a single sound could be heard, save for a night breeze sweeping down from the open ceiling above him. In the darkness, in the silence, he found himself alone. Not just physically, but emotionally. Even mentally. The absence of not only Jessica, the other women, or even the facility itself, but also the absence of Cynthia from his life seemed to suddenly grate on him.

Harvey pushed through the emotional turmoil and replayed Jessica's route in his mind.

He attacked the maze again. This time, he managed to navigate himself to the center clearing Jessica had led him to earlier. The podium stood, with the Maddening Marigold corsage still in place upon it. The four benches were there as well, only one of them had a square of paper sitting on the edge.

He glanced around the clearing, flashing his light around the hedges. He saw nothing out of the ordinary. The mist seemed to be growing thicker, seeping into the clearing from the various paths of the maze.

Harvey approached the bench and saw that the piece of paper was actually a photograph. He took a seat and picked up the photo. It was of a man and woman having dinner with one another. Harvey recognized both of them. One by their face, the other by their hair and the framework of their body.

The man was Victor Paxton, the murder victim that Harvey had been getting text messages from the VFPD about all night, and the other was Cerena Hatcher—Carnation.

He flipped the photo over.

Victor Paxton & Cerena Hatcher
Valentine's Day 2021

SO IN LOVE – Why?

So, Cerena was having an affair with Augustine's husband, Harvey thought. *Something must have gone awry to cause Cerena to kill him.*

Harvey slid the photo into the inside pocket of his coat. He bundled the front of his coat. He had to call the Midnight City Police Department and have them put an arrest out for Cerena Hatcher. He wasn't sure if she was even still on the grounds of the Gardens, but at least making it official would give Harvey some peace of mind. He wasn't sure if any of the women were still on the grounds. Most likely, they all scattered and used the time he had been trapped out here to escape the Gardens and flee back to their elitist strongholds.

He turned and grabbed the corsage of the Madding Marigold off the podium. He would need to start collecting as much evidence as he could to prove his case against Cerena—and whoever else might be involved in this.

He pulled out his phone but found there to be no signal in the middle of the hedge maze. Cursing under his breath, he shoved the phone in his pocket and started to make his way back through the labyrinth of foliage.

The fog had grown significantly thicker, making it somewhat difficult to see the signs clearly. He knew he would have to navigate backwards to get out: YBOR. Yellow, blue, orange, and red. He made a right, a left, then another right. Then he realized he was right back in the center with the benches and the podium. He exited again, this time left, then right, then another right. He entered a corridor of hedges that seemed to go on forever, thick fog creating a carpet at his feet. As he charged down the aisle of plants, he heard a soft voice. A woman's voice.

Cynthia's voice.

"Harvey. Come here and let me fix that tie."

He swung around to see who was behind him, but there was nothing but fog. He swung back around, pulling his weapon from its holster. Nobody. Just fog.

"Show yourself!" he shouted to the air.

"Don't be silly, Harvey. If I don't fix your tie, you'll embarrass the both of us."

The fog started to move toward him. Covering him. Smothering him…

Chapter 19

"Harvey, you aren't going anywhere until I straighten your tie."

He opened his eyes. Warmth engulfed him. The heater was blowing hot air down on him from the vent in the apartment ceiling.

Cynthia came around the corner from the next room. She wore a stunning black and gold dress, tight around the hips and breast, and flared at the bottom like a beautiful bell. Her long black hair had a few curls spun into her bangs, while the rest flowed freely down her back, ending near her waistline.

She looked perturbed.

Harvey felt…disoriented. There was something not right about this.

She marched over to him, taking hold of his thin black tie. "Are you deaf, Harvey Elder? I've been mentioning your tie for the last five minutes, and I come in here and find you standing around, doing close to nothing but breathing."

He inhaled the sweet smell of rose perfume, mixed with the unmistakable scent of foundation makeup. Cynthia had dolled herself up in blush and bright red lipstick, adding decent accessories to her beautiful brown eyes.

She looked up at him and frowned. "Seriously, why do you

look like you're lost in a haze?"

He shrugged. He could feel the tight suit jacket pulling at his shoulders as he did so. "Sor...Sorry." His throat felt scratchy, dry.

She finished adjusting his tie—nearly choking him to death—then stomped away, her two-inch heels prodding the white carpet as they brought her back to the room she had exited from. "I need you to be on your best behavior tonight, Harvey. This isn't a brothel or a downtown bar. This is the Scars Feed, the most elegant restaurant in Midnight City.

He sighed. He hated the Scars Feed. Only elites seemed to dine there. He wasn't an elite. Neither was Cynthia. She worked in corporate America, selling insurance. He...well, he used to be a great detective. Now he was a private investigator solving Nancy Drew type mysteries while his girlfriend helped him make ends meet.

"I heard that sigh of contempt. I know you don't want to go tonight. Too bad. It's time I show you off to my friends. They've been asking about who my 'wonderful beau' is, and so you'll be taking center stage this evening. Be on your best."

Something about this...felt familiar. Felt real. What was he doing here? Where had he been before he opened his eyes?

He glanced down at his suit. Black coat and pants. White shirt. Black tie. Very boring. Plain. Dull. He felt like all he was missing was a pair of black sunglasses and then he could go explore the site of an alien crash.

Cynthia reentered the room, grabbing her purse off the counter. Harvey noticed the fridge was covered in magnets from all over the world. He glanced around and found the walls of his apartment to be covered in paintings of Italian landscapes and plants. So many plants. In her spare time, Cynthia loved to garden—which she did at her house in the suburbs—but he had no interest in plants. In flowers. In anything to do with botany.

Cynthia stood at the counter and narrowed her eyes on him. "What is your problem? You high on something?"

He shook his head, straightened his jacket, and started toward her.

"Good." She said as she pulled a set of keys from her purse.

She drove them to the Scars Feed. It was a thirty-minute journey, fighting Friday night traffic into the heart of Midnight City. The restaurant was located on the third story of the Reese building.

The long drive passed like a blur to Harvey. He felt as if it was a gap, a dark patch, of memory. What did he do in the car while she drove? What music was on the radio? What other cars or what other parts of Midnight City did he see?

He couldn't remember, couldn't conjure any of it.

After addressing the hostess, Cynthia tugged Harvey toward a corner table where three women sat.

The women were dressed in fine gowns and dolled up in makeup and jewelry. Cynthia pulled Harvey toward the table and motioned to him as if she were Vanna White on Wheel of Fortune. "And this, ladies, is my boyfriend, Harvey Elder."

The woman all nodded and waved at him. One woman in particular, dressed in a blue gown, raised her eyebrows at him. "*The* Harvey Elder? The one who was in the papers for the death of Lindsay Eves?"

Harvey shifted his stance and decided to take a seat in the chair across from the women. Cynthia sat to the left of him.

"Yes," he said. "It was all—"

"A misunderstanding," the woman finished. "I know. I followed that story almost obsessively."

"Strange," Cynthia said.

The woman laughed. "Not really. I had been following Harvey's career for years before that. He is a noted detective. One who sees what others do not."

Cynthia scoffed. "Yeah. If he was such a noted detective, explain why he lives in an apartment and can only find work solving cases of infidelity."

The woman ignored Cynthia's comment and made eye contact with Harvey again. "I appreciate your work. You have a certain...panache...toward things."

Harvey nodded. He couldn't help but allow a grin to creep along his face. He turned to Cynthia, and her eyes scolded him.

"Anyway, Winter, what brings you here tonight?" Cynthia said, addressing the woman in the blue dress. The other two women seemed disinterested in the conversation and were chatting among themselves. "I invited you tonight, but you declined, saying you had to head to the Pleasure District to run an errand."

Winter smiled, not at Cynthia, but at Harvey. "I did. Managed to get back here in time to meet your lovely detective boyfriend."

"He's not a detective anymore. He's a private investigator."

Winter took a long sip of what looked like wine and shrugged. "Once a detective, always a detective. Right?"

Harvey reluctantly nodded.

"I have family in law-enforcement. I, myself, have no interest in participating in it. However, I enjoy hearing her stories about all the crazy stuff that goes on in Midnight City."

Harvey smiled nervously at her. There was something about her. Something that seemed familiar.

"I will kill you, Harvey Elder."

He turned, thinking Cynthia had said those words. But she was drinking from her glass of wine. He glanced at the other women at the table, but the two who were chatting with one another were still doing so, completely ignoring him and even Cynthia. Winter though was staring directly at him, sipping from her wine glass.

"Who said that?"

"Said what?" Cynthia asked.

The loud commotion in the room started to fade.

"I will kill you, Harvey Elder. I must...kill you."

"Who said that?" He stood up from the table and glanced around the room. Nobody seemed to stick out to him. A feeling of utter déjà vu hit him, and he looked down at Cynthia. She looked up at him, her head shaking at the shame of her boyfriend losing his mind.

"We're going to chop you up into little pieces and spread you throughout the Gardens."

He stumbled backwards, knocking his chair back to the floor.

Cynthia stood, tossing the napkin she had been keeping on her lap to the table, as if it had caused her some great dishonor. "What the hell are you doing? Sit down before you embarrass yourself any further."

He looked at Winter. Her eyes remained focused on him over her wineglass. Her blue-painted nails barely touched the glass. Then, suddenly, blood started to seep out of her eyes. Her wineglass shattered, and blood splashed across the table.

She continued to look up at him as if nothing unusual was happening. "You let me die, detective. You let them kill me. I was the one you could trust. Now who can you trust?"

Cynthia seemed to take no notice of the blood everywhere. Harvey stepped backwards, bumping into a waiter who was moving with a tray throughout the room. The tray flipped over, and plates of food flung into the air, landing all over the dining area.

Cynthia stomped her foot against the floor. "Get out of here, Harvey! Get out! You've embarrassed me for the last time!"

"You're a fine soul to feed the gardens. Your body, your flesh, your blood, will settle in the soil and make our plants—our children—grow and grow. And grow."

Harvey shut his eyes, scratching at them, screaming to wake up from whatever nightmare he had found himself in.

He felt a cold chill surround him, draining any heat he had felt in the restaurant.

Chapter 20

When he opened his eyes, a cloaked figure stood over him, the suffocating blackness of the fabric nearly blocking his view of the hedges behind them. The figure held a knife in their right hand and were mid-swing before Harvey realized what was going on and rolled to his right.

The knife came down into the lawn, and the figure stood there, like a robot for a moment, before pulling the knife out of the ground. They stood up straight and then turned toward him, taking another swing.

Harvey scrambled to his feet, shifted to the right—avoiding the swing of the blade, and then went for his revolver. The gun was gone. He padded his pockets and found the photo and his phone gone as well. His money, however, was still there.

"Who are you?" he asked as he pulled the corsage of the Maddening Magnolia from his pocket. The petals felt oily, grainy. He tossed the corsage to the ground and wiped his fingers on his pants.

The cloaked entity said nothing. Harvey could tell by the slender figure that this was a woman who was trying to kill him. He tried to glance a peek under the hood of the cloak, but all he saw was a black mask disguising any facial features.

She took another swing at him, but he easily ducked out of

the way. She went through the same robotic motions again, giving Harvey time to observe her actions, her figure, her very presence.

The cloak came up about ten inches from the bottom of the black flat soles she wore. He saw no marks on her ankles. *This isn't Lilac, who had the tattoo on her left ankle.* She swung again, left-handed, and this time it came quicker. He shifted to his left, but the knife managed to skate across his shoulder, slicing a small incision through his coat. Another swing, this time missing him altogether as she plunged the knife into the hedges. As she tried to pull it free from the foliage, he noticed her bare arms and the absence of any jewelry on her fingers.

That means this isn't Tina with the ring, or Marigold with the fancy watch.

Another cloaked figure came down from the top of the hedges. Harvey managed to spot them in time to move to his right. A knife came down past the side of his face as the new attacker landed on the lawn and rolled to an upright position.

Two attackers, one on each side of him. His gun would have come in handy right about now.

Unfortunately, the first one who had attacked him was blocking his exit from the maze.

The one behind him swung the knife dangerously close to his head. He ducked, and the blade slid through the hairs on his head.

He pressed his back into the hedge wall and faced the two of them.

The slow-moving, robotic one swung at him again, but this time he rolled under the blade and managed to come out behind her.

He ran.

Thoughts flashed through his mind as he did his best to remember his way out of the labyrinth. Yellow, blue, orange, red. Through twists and turns, he charged his way through, never once chancing a glance over his shoulder to see if either one of the cloaked attackers were following.

As he ran, he noticed the corridors growing thinner. He rubbed his eyes, wondering if he was still under the influence of the Maddening Marigold. The hedge hallways thinned in an attempt to block his path or crush him.

He raced faster, his mind going into autopilot, relaying the directions he knew deep in his subconscious to get out of the maze. His vision seemed blurred at the edges, making it hard to see clearly.

He swung around a corner and spotted the hedge archway, running through it, exiting the maze. He rushed past the Venus flytraps, careful to give them clearance as their jowls snapped at him. He rubbed his eyes and took another look, realizing the flytraps weren't moving at all. Past the flytraps, he entered the Flora Tunnel, lit with bioluminescent light that seeped from the flowers growing in the ceiling of the archway. He ran as his mind tried to force itself upon his reality, making it seem as if the glowing tunnel was squeezing together in an attempt to suffocate him in flowers. It certainly wasn't the way he wanted to die. He always imagined dying in a gun fight, or heroically saving someone's life. Not having his final breath smothered from him by plants.

He closed his eyes, took a deep, exhausted breath, and opened them to see that nothing out of the ordinary was actually occurring with the tunnel. It stood, unmoving, as he passed through it.

When he reached the end, he stopped to catch his breath. He peered behind him, seeing nothing but the long, arched corridor of glowing plants staring back at him. The Gardens seemed alive, teeming with hostility toward him. But he knew it was all in his head. The aftereffects of the Magnolia.

He stood there, keeled over, panting, as he gave his mind time to recover from the effects of the hallucinogenic flower. He tried to take a quick, mental inventory of his situation. He had no phone, which meant he had no way of calling out to the Midnight City Police Department. He was trapped within the Gardens, meaning he was at the mercy of whoever was playing these games. And spread throughout the Gardens were strange plants that had the power to undo him if he wasn't more careful.

He turned and continued along the purple-stoned path, hoping not to trip in the darkness. His vision started to clear up a little, with the blurriness now turning into a faint haze, like mist at the edges of his vision. The moon hung overhead, giving him just enough light to make his way through the gardens and back to the entryway to the foyer—which was still shut, but was now covered in thick vines.

He tried to claw his way through the foliage, but the vines were too thick, shielding the door—and the building itself—from outsiders. He peered through the window to the left of the doors and saw that the hallways and the rest of the building were empty.

Where was Jessica? Where were the rest of the women?

He turned expecting to find the attackers, but the gardens were suddenly dead silent. Harvey could hear his own lungs struggling to catch up to him, and the burning moved throughout his chest and up his throat. He leaned over again, trying to catch his breath. He wondered if his trouble breathing was caused by the Magnolia.

His mind tried to bother him, tried to nudge him and annoy him into trying to put all of the pieces together, but he wanted nothing more now than to escape the Gardens. He had no way back out to the parking lot—unless he could try to scale the wall of the botanical gardens. He was fairly certain Augustine would have crafted the walls high enough to prevent such a thing.

Harvey took a seat on the cement flooring and leaned his back against the door. His vision felt...fuzzy. Blurry. His mind and heart raced. He took more deep breaths to calm himself. Something wasn't right. He glanced down at his hand—the one that had taken hold of the Magnolia. Under the pale moonlight and the glow from the hallway lighting peering out of the windows, he saw darkened discoloration on his skin. Even his pants had the darkened color.

The memory of Cynthia...it had felt so real. He was actually there. The memory wasn't complete though. In the memory, by just standing in the living room of his apartment, dumbfounded, he had initiated conversation with Cynthia that hadn't actually happened. Other than that, everything went almost exactly to memory. Except for the ending.

He remembered now, meeting Winter at that dinner date. Of course, her eyes hadn't bled and there hadn't been so much commotion at that dinner table. No, Cynthia had insulted his profession. Constantly. So constantly in fact, that he snapped and told her off at that table.

That's what led to their breakup. That's what led to everything going downhill.

But did she have a right to criticize his profession?

No.

Henry took another deep breath. His lungs still burned, but the pain was subsiding. His heart rate slowed a bit. His vision finally cleared up.

He had never wanted to admit the issues with Cynthia. She had been the only one to care for him in a very, very long time. But had it all been a farce? They were from two separate worlds. She came from a more 'dignified' background, while he had always lived in the margins, barely scraping by.

Was it all about money?

He heard noises in the Garden, in the direction of the hedge maze. Rustling noises. Soft voices, talking.

He struggled to his feet and reached for his gun, forgetting briefly that he didn't have it.

Two figures stepped out onto the purple-stoned path that led out of the Flora Tunnel. From where Harvey stood—and with help from the moonlight—he could tell they weren't cloaked. It was two of the women, still dressed in their elaborate ball gowns.

He was sure he could probably defend himself, but he didn't want to go another round without his firearm.

"Detective," the one on the left said as they approached him. Chrysanthemum. She wore a long, black fur-coat that went to the ground.

Lilac stood beside her, with what looked like a large gash in her right arm. Her dress was torn at the sleeve, blood leaking down her arm as she held it with her good hand. "Well, looks like we all ran into a bit of trouble out here in the gardens."

"What happened to you?" Harvey asked.

Lilac smirked. "Nothing I couldn't handle."

Chrysanthemum put a hand to her chest. "Detective, something is out there in the Gardens. If you hadn't noticed."

"Yeah, I've noticed," he said.

"It would seem the Gardens are alive, but we know that's not possible. Still...Lilac here got caught in a tangle of thorns. Shredded her coat and left their mark on her."

Lilac gripped her wounded arm. "I need a bit of aid, detective, if you don't mind." She pointed to a first aid kit that was attached to the wall to the side of the sealed door.

Harvey rushed over and opened the kit and started on wrapping Lilac's wound. The woman was thinner and frailer than he had at first realized. Each of these women were turning out to be something else entirely different than what he had first assumed.

Lilac sat on the cement. After Harvey wrapped her wound, Chrysanthemum narrowed her eyes on him. "Why would you help her?"

Harvey let out a long breath. "Why wouldn't I?"

"We're suspects. Not your friends."

He let out a quick chuckle. "Suspect doesn't equal enemy."

"We have many enemies," Chrysanthemum said.

"As do I," Harvey replied. "And not just women," he joked.

Lilac reached up and pulled off her mask, setting it on the ground next to her. By the light of the hallway, her features looked aged, but her face had developed a sort of grace over the years. With her full features available for him to see, Harvey now saw slyness and wit in her eyes. Crows feet spread from the corners of her eyes and added a trail of years to her features.

"Detective, you probably know who we are by now."

Harvey nodded. "Auburn Simpson." He turned to Chrysanthemum. "Tina Redfield."

They both looked at each other, not at all surprised. Then they looked at him.

"We need you to put an end to this," Tina said. "We think one of the other women are out to kill us."

Harvey craved a cigarette. Maybe a few of them. "Who?"

They both shrugged.

"We don't know, detective," Tina answered. "We know it isn't us."

Harvey smiled. "How do I know it isn't one—or both—of you?"

Tina and Auburn laughed.

"We've lived long lives, Detective," Lilac said with a grin.

Tina slid off her mask. Her features were much more worn than Auburn's. Tina's face held scars, and she looked as if she had a burn mark on the left side of her cheekbone, where the mask had covered it up. "Auburn and I are good friends. Have been for many, many years."

Auburn rubbed the bandaged arm. "I don't have it in me to pursue things of this diabolical nature anymore. I've found I really just want to settle down. Enjoy my life. But it seems Tina and I found our way into an organization that doesn't want us doing so."

"The Order of the Vine," Harvey whispered.

Auburn smiled.

Tina raised an eyebrow. "You're smarter than I thought you were."

"Thanks?" Harvey said. "And for what it's worth, I know neither one of you were the ones who attacked me in the hedge maze."

"Attacked you?"

He nodded, standing to his feet. "There's two robed people running around out there. One of them tried to kill me when I was under the influence of the Maddening Magnolia. The other attacked me when I was defending myself from the first one. I think I know who's behind all of this."

"You think it's Cerena Hatcher," Tina said.

Harvey nodded.

"We both think there's more to it than that. We know Cerena. She's not into killing people."

Auburn stood up, holding her arm and groaning while she did it. Once she was standing still, she took a deep breath. "Detective—Harvey—Cerena lost her baby some time ago.

She's been devastated ever since. She came here because she was invited, by Augustine, to participate in this looney auction. All of us were invited."

"I have reason to believe she was having an affair with Augustine's husband. And that she stole the death rose and used it to kill him. At least, that's what it looks like. There are just pieces of the puzzle I'm missing."

Tina shook her head. "We're telling you, Cerena didn't do this. At least, not by choice."

"Whoever attacked me in that maze had to be one of the other three women: Augustine, Jessica, or Cerena. That narrows things down significantly."

"Wait a minute," Tina said. "What about Marigold and Winter."

"Winter is dead," Harvey said.

"What?" Auburn looked genuinely shocked.

Tina slapped her palms against her legs. "I knew it. I knew it!"

"Knew what?"

A gunshot rang out, and blood splattered across the sealed doorway of the foyer. Auburn stumbled backwards, eyes wide, and fell to the ground.

Harvey dove toward her, crouching in a shielding position to protect her from another shot as Tina stood, frozen, facing the cloaked woman who was approaching them, pistol in hand.

Harvey's pistol.

"I have to kill you three. Cut you up. Make you part of the Gardens."

"Cerena," Harvey said.

The cloaked figure shifted their head up. He still couldn't see her face because of the black mask, but he was certain it was Cerena by the tone of her voice and the stature of her figure.

Tina put her hands in the air. "Cerena, dear, put the gun down."

Harvey risked a glance down long enough to see that Auburn had been shot in the chest. Blood blossomed through the front of her dress. Her eyes stared up at him for a moment before she gave up her final breath and died in his arms.

He looked up at Cerena, who was still pointing his gun at Tina. "Cerena. Honey. You need to put the gun down. You need to come back to us, okay?"

Harvey set Auburn gently on the ground. There wasn't anything he could do for her now. She had no pulse—the bullet had hit her straight through the heart. *His* bullet. From *his* gun.

He stood to his feet, slowly, as Cerena turned the gun on him.

"You have been a nuisance, Detective Elder. She says you must die. It has to end here."

Harvey put his hands in the air and took an almost imperceptible step toward her. With her mask on, Cerena wasn't going to be able to have the range of sight or motion that Harvey and Tina had.

He lunged to the right as Cerena's gun moved in that direction, then he faked and darted to the left, striking the arm that held the gun. She dropped the weapon as it tumbled behind Harvey, clattering into the sealed door.

Harvey struck Cerena in the back of the neck, knocking her like a rag doll. She wobbled a bit, then fell to the ground, catching herself on her hands.

Tina rushed to the Cerena's aid. She pulled back the woman's hood and removed her mask. Brunette hair spilled out over her face. The girl struggled, slapping Tina with her hands, kicking her feet as the cloak and her hair flailed around like a shadow being.

Harvey thought to grab his gun, but Cerena's fingerprints were all over it. It was proof he needed to prove Cerena had been the active killer in this. Instead, he approached Cerena and helped Tina hold the girl down.

"Get off me! Get off me, please, you're hurting me!"

Harvey grabbed her hands and held them in front of her, pulling her to a sitting up position. "Cerena. We're not going to hurt you."

Tina slapped Cerena across the cheek. "Pull yourself together!"

Tears streamed from Cerena's eyes, and it was then that Harvey noticed, through the curtain of dark hair, the strange orange dots in her white pupils.

"Take off her robe," he said to Tina.

She gave him a look, but he insisted, nodding his head toward Cerena. "Trust me."

Tina unfurled the tie at the waist of the robe and pulled the front flaps open. Cerena wore a white T-shirt and white shorts. But a poppy corsage was pinned to her chest.

Harvey saw the same orange petals on the corsage that he had been seeing all night. He used part of the robe to cover his hands and then gently removed the corsage through the sharp pin at the back that was affixing it to her shirt.

"We all had one of those corsages when we arrived here tonight," Tina whispered.

Harvey nodded. He removed the corsage and set it on the ground next to him. *Another piece of proof.* "I know. You all had fakes, supposedly."

Cerena's eyes rolled into the back of her head, and her breathing suddenly returned to normal as Tina and Harvey helped her onto her back so she could lay on the ground. She fell asleep immediately.

Harvey turned to Tina. "Someone else is behind all of this."

Tina nodded. "Jessica? Augustine?" She stepped over to Auburn's body there on the concrete. "She was a good friend of mine. She wasn't a troublemaker. Not really." She knelt down and put her hand on Auburn's forehead. "I loved her like a sister."

Harvey watched the Gardens. Silence. "I'm sorry. I really am. But right now, we have to find out who is behind this and stop them. Maybe Marigold—"

"No." Auburn shook her head. Harvey could hear her trying to hold back tears. "Auburn and I watched her march through the lobby and head to her car. She said she didn't want any part in this. That you were a pig, and that Augustine was a fool to allow this nonsense to happen in her gardens."

Harvey rubbed his chin. "That leaves two suspects."

Tina nodded. "Jessica and Augustine."

"Or both."

Tina took a deep breath. "If Auburn and I had left with Marigold…Auburn would still be alive."

Harvey put his hand on her shoulder. "I need your help to finish this."

She nodded, took hold of Auburn's hand, then closed her eyes as she whispered a prayer.

Harvey wasn't sure how to get out of the Gardens. He needed his phone. Needed a gun that wasn't plastered with a killer's fingerprints.

He remembered Jessica mentioning an entrance into the laboratory area from the gardens themselves, but it was clear on the other side through a menagerie of plant-themed areas.

He looked over at the window and realized he could probably break the glass. That would get everyone's attention, maybe even trigger an alarm to get the police down here.

He went to the stone pathway and lifted one of the purple cobblestones out of it. The ground was reluctant to give up its treasure, and Harvey had to dig his fingers underneath the stone to pry it loose.

"What are you doing?" Tina asked as she stood to her feet.

"Going to break that window," he said as he lifted the stone into his hands and started toward the window. "Get us into the building." He hefted the stone in both hands and then cast it toward the glass panel. The stone hit the surface, bounced off, and fell straight to the ground, chipping the concrete.

Harvey ran his dirt-covered hands through his hair. "You've got to be kidding me."

"Seems the glass doesn't like you either," Tina said.

With there being no way back into the building going this way, he motioned toward the area of the Gardens just beyond the gazebo. "We need to get through the lab."

"What do we do with her?" Tina asked, motioning to Cerena.

Harvey stepped on the poppy corsage, crushing it under his foot. Then he kicked it off into a bush. "She'll be fine. She's probably going to sleep the effects off. Hopefully." He took a cloth out of his pocket and used it to lift his gun from the ground. He wrapped it in the cloth and shoved it into his pocket. "You and I need to get out of the Gardens. I get the feeling we aren't welcome here—by anyone."

Tina straightened out her green dress and pulled her fur coat closed. "I'll help you as much as I can."

He nodded, feeling as though he could trust Tina. He reminded himself not to. These women had been playing games with him most of the night. Though he was inclined to believe Tina and Auburn's claims of innocence in all of this, he needed

Chapter 21

H arvey led Tina back toward the gazebo. He brought them around it, to the other side, along the purple-stoned path. He had to use moonlight, as he had lost his flashlight earlier in the maze. The moon in its full glory was enough to light the path in front of them, but the light was eerie, soundless. It gave the gardens a life Harvey didn't want it to have, gave it breath he didn't think it deserved.

He and Tina remained close to each other's side. The sound of rushing water could be heard as he led them in the direction he remembered the lab being in according to his time in the building. The sound of rushing water grew louder as the pathway's purple color seemed to fade into a mute green, and the vegetation on the sides of the pathway turned from bright, floral groupings to vibrant, green stems and stalks.

They reached another archway, this one made of stone, leading them into a large courtyard. A massive stone fountain depicting an oak tree stood in the center, spewing water out into its large circular basin. The area was covered in lush green lawn, and tall trees surrounded the area. These trees seemed to have a greenish glow to them as light softly emitted from their bark.

Harvey watched as Tina approached one of the trees and

reached her hand out to it, pressing her palm against the bark.

"Isn't it amazing," she said, "to think Midnight City could create something so beautiful?"

"You think these are natural?"

"It's highly likely. I've studied many plants in my lifetime, and I can't recall coming across anything like glowing bark. It's possible Augustine created these through some strange botany, but I doubt it. I know through my research that Midnight City is a hub for the strange…and the phenomenal."

"Tell me more about The Order of the Vine."

She shook her head. "I can't. I am sworn to secrecy. You know it exists. That's more than most people can say. I can tell you that my involvement in it is purely for research and preservation purposes. I care about the plants…not the money, not the power."

"What about you?"

"What about me?"

"I know near to nothing—really—about any of you."

"Should you? I love plants. That's the focus of my life."

"Not the husband you don't really have?"

Tina looked at him with narrowed eyes. "The ring gave it away, ironically enough, didn't it?"

Harvey nodded. "No tan line. The way you spoke of your 'husband.' You're single. And your focus is indeed on plants."

She nodded as she ran her fingers along the stone basin of the fountain. "My late husband 'fell' off a skyrise. I'm pretty sure it was members of Midnight City's drug cartel who killed him. I genuinely loved him. He was my better half, for sure. After his death, I decided to turn from crime. Opened up a string of herbalist shops throughout the city. I have two of them still. Had to sell the others because the cartel came knocking on my door, demanding I pay them 'protection fees.'"

Harvey knew of the cartel. They went by many different names throughout Midnight City, depending on who was dealing with them. He knew them as the Syndicate. They were really just a small-time gang that rose in the ranks via outrageously violent intimidations and reckless thefts.

"Mr. Elder, I would like to get out of this place now, if you please."

He looked into Tina's eyes and saw tears streaming down her face. He nodded to her. He too wanted to leave this place. It felt as if he was walking through a graveyard of memories.

He looked down into the fountain's basin. The water had chunks of glowing bark floating in it. The liquid itself was teal colored, making it so he couldn't see to the bottom of the basin.

Tina marveled at the floating bark. "Magnificent." She reached her hand into the water.

Something tugged on her hand and pulled her toward the fountain. "Hey!" She used her other hand to grab the edge of the basin and stop herself from falling in.

Harvey grabbed her shoulders from the back and tried to pull her away from the water.

"Something's wrapped around my wrist! It won't let...eh...go!" She struggled against whatever was inside the water as Harvey reached his hand into the liquid at the place her wrist was caught.

The water itself felt thick, oily. It tingled his skin just slightly, like a weak electrical current. He reached his fingers around whatever had grabbed her. He felt tendrils—or vines—under the water, tight around her wrist. He tried to pry them free, but they were too strong and too slippery. He glanced around the courtyard but could find nothing that he could use to cut Tina loose. He pulled and scraped at the vines while Tina continued to try and tug herself free.

She finally managed to wrestle free and then stumbled backwards, falling to the ground on her back.

Harvey pulled his hands out of the water and stepped away from the fountain. He turned and helped Tina to her feet.

"What was that?" she asked as she stood. She examined her wrist. Long red marks wrapped around her skin, and bruising had already begun around those marks. "What are those?!"

Harvey drew close to the fountain. He carefully tried to peer into the water where her arm had gotten nabbed by something, afraid of getting caught himself. The water was cloudy from their disturbance, but now he was able to see through to the bottom of the fountain basin in one particular spot. He saw a shimmer—nothing more—which seemed to reflect the glowing bark that was floating along the surface of the water. The same glimmer he remembered seeing earlier in the investigation.

"Invisible Vines."

He heard Tina let out a string of foul words. Then she kicked her foot into the lawn, digging up a giant chunk of sod. She kicked it with the tip of her heel, and it shot into the air as bits of dirt sprinkled down into the fountain water.

Harvey pointed to the tall, glowing trees. "I think once we pass through these, we'll find the door to the laboratory."

Tina huffed. "Great. Who the hell knows what Augustine hid in there?"

Harvey nodded. "I know. But once we get into the lab, I can get to a phone and bring the police down on this place."

Tina's face lit up. "The police?"

He nodded again. "Yeah. There's been two murders. The police have to be called."

"The police will find our connection with The Order of the

Vine."

Harvey started toward the line of trees, tempted to bring some of the glowing bark from the fountain with him. There were items around the Gardens that most likely could have fetched a handsome price on the black market. Though he hadn't delved into that area in a while, he could make enough to move him someplace more respectable.

But is that me?

He wasn't even sure he himself had asked that question. Some deep, dark part of his inner consciousness asked it, curious if he was doing all that he was to change Cynthia's mind about leaving him.

But what if I wanted her to leave me?

That question caught him off guard.

"Harvey—Detective—whatever you want to be called! Did you hear me?"

He put a hand up to stop her tantrum and then stopped in front of the line of trees. There was a frigid cold breeze escaping the small copse. It made him shiver, but he knew just beyond this thicket was the laboratory. Once he reached it, he could figure out how to break into the building. Then, once he was inside, he could put an end to all of this.

"I heard you. I don't plan on revealing The Order of the Vine. At least, not your part in it."

Tina threw her hands up. "My part? If you reveal *anyone's* part, they'll find the links that lead back to me."

Harvey stepped across the threshold of the tiny forest.

He heard Tina scream, and then turned to find a massive cluster of vines sweep up from the fountain and wrap around her. She struggled and writhed as the vines covered her whole body up to her head. She screamed, but her voice was muffled by a rumbling sound coming from underneath Harvey's feet. The ground shook, and Harvey struggled to keep his balance as the trees themselves started to move their branches, creating a wall in front of him, completely blocking his path back to the fountain.

When the rumbling stopped, a glowing branch wall stood solid in between Harvey and Tina.

He reached out to touch it, but a vine branch swung out and slapped his hand, slicing his skin.

Harvey shoved his wound into his mouth, tasting blood.

He turned back to the small forest standing between him and the lab. He felt panic creeping in, knowing Tina was in danger but having no way of helping her. Of even helping himself, really. Would whoever was behind this kill her too?

He took a deep breath. The forest was engulfed in the unnatural glow from the tree bark, giving the area a soft, greenish hue. He peered up, hoping to see sky, hoping to catch sight of the moon, but he only caught sight of more darkness as he noticed the glowing bark dimmed to black as it reached closer to the tops of the trees.

A well-worn dirt path beckoned him, one that weaved through the trees. One that hopefully led to the Augustine's laboratory.

Chapter 22

As he wandered through the glowing trees, Harvey tried to keep his wits about him. He didn't have an entourage of cult-following women with him any longer. He didn't have Jessica there to guide him through the gardens. He didn't have Cynthia there to guide him through his mess of a life.

He was alone. And that aloneness felt...liberating.

The forest was abuzz with the sounds of night. Crickets chirped. Woodland creatures scurried across the path back and forth in front of him. Most of them squirrels, but he caught a glimpse of a skunk at one point.

The air itself was full of oxygen—full of life. It filled his lungs and refreshed his spirit.

Ever since he had fallen as a detective, because of Lindsay Eve's death, he had thought—believed even—that his life, at the very least his career, was over. It had been the ultimate bottom-of-the-barrel moment for him.

When he decided to return to private investigation, Cynthia entered his life. He thought she meant to come alongside him and help him to blossom back into his detective role again.

He was wrong.

What would she think of him taking on this case? He wondered if it would make her take him more seriously.

So what if she does or doesn't? Does it matter?

Harvey supposed not. Not now. Not after the way she treated him.

I'll always love you, Cynthia, he told himself. *In some way.*

The very words in his head felt gross. Unnatural. And he wasn't sure why.

The ground under his feet was soft. Almost too soft. The soil felt somewhat slippery. Oily. He realized everything felt oily. The plants. The petals. The soil. Was there something about the oil? Where did it come from? Was it natural? Was it from the Twilight Tulip that Jessica had mentioned to him earlier? She had said Augustine used the oil from the Tulip in her research, because of its special properties. Was the oil the reason for all of this plant life that broke the rules of nature?

The path wound through the trees, but there seemed to be no end to the trees themselves. Strangely enough, Harvey felt he had been walking for at least a half mile—and the gardens weren't even that big.

Impossible.

He stopped. *Impossible? All of this is impossible. Glowing bark, glowing flowers, invisible plants, plants that play with your mind. Roses that kill.*

Nothing seemed impossible at this point. He had already seen crazy things throughout his time in Midnight City. But now this? This only added to all of it.

He wanted to continue down the path through the trees, but something told him it was all a trick. The path was the trick. He broke from the path and started to maneuver his way through the trees themselves.

The glow from the bark guided his route, but he could sense the trees moving their branches. He wasn't sure if they were getting ready for another 'attack,' or if they were 'allowing' him to move through the copse unharmed.

He weaved through the thicket and managed to finally reach the main building. The door to the laboratory stood at the end of the route he had taken—not the end of the path. He didn't even know where the path had gone.

He approached the blue steel door and the keycard reader to the right of the door frame. He had no keycard, no password either. He reached into his coat to see if his lockpick kit was still there, see if he could maybe use it to short-circuit the code panel. It wasn't.

He watched with some surprise as the red glowing light on the keycard reader flashed green, and a familiar clunk sounded from within the door.

Chapter 23

H arvey entered the warm laboratory, half-expecting Augustine to be standing, gun in hand, ready to meet him, and help him meet his maker.

Instead, he found the room somewhat silent, save for the distinct sound of glass clinking against glass. The room was enormous, but most of it was taken up by large racks of planters, all filled with various foliage. Heat lamps shined down on them, and he could see there was a small watering system installed above each one to hydrate the plants.

To his left, he saw a wall covered in vines that seemed to slither like snakes. He made sure to stay away from it, so he didn't wind up like Tina.

Dozens of lab counters and tables were lines up along the walls of the lab, each covered in beakers and vials and plants. Diagrams sketched out on old papyrus covered some of the walls, drawings that looked to be of the plants within the gardens. Most of them though were sketches of the Twilight Tulip, but he also recognized the Death Rose, the Invisible Vines, and the Maddening Marigold.

As Harvey slowly and cautiously made his way through the laboratory in the hopes of finding Augustine or at least finding a phone, he passed between the walls of planters. The air was thick and musty. There was a floral scent, but there was also the smell of alcohol—the kind used to clean lab equipment. Once he passed through the planters, he found an individual sitting at a lab counter, fiddling with some beakers full of dark liquid. A sketch of the Bewitching Poppy was plastered to the wall above her.

Her long blonde hair came down below the seat of the chair, covering most of her white lab coat. She wore black heels on her feet, and white gloves on her hands.

"Ah, Detective Harvey Elder."

Harvey wanted badly to pull his gun on this woman. He knew, deep in his gut, she had been the perpetrator of his entire messed up evening.

She swirled the beaker in her hand, watching the liquid slosh around in the glass, then set the vial down on the counter and looked at Harvey. "Speechless?"

He noticed other vials lined up against the wall, labels above each of them: Naloxone, Anticholinesterase, Pralidoxime, Perezine, Atropine, Dimercaprol. The vial for the Perezine was missing. A landline phone—an old rotary model—sat off to the side, teasing him with its presence.

"You're under arrest for the murder of Winter Jackson and Auburn Simpson."

"Murder? Me?" Augustine stood to her feet and started pulling her gloves off. Her eyes remained focused on her hands, but there was a smirk growing on her lips, and her hazel-colored eyes seemed to be playing with him. "My dear Harvey, you have me confused with someone else. I wouldn't hurt the hair on a fly's head."

"I have proof." He said the words, but realized the proof he had implicated Cerena Hatcher, not Augustine.

She paused and raised an eyebrow at him. "Do you?"

He said nothing more.

"That's what I thought," she said as she finished taking her gloves off. "You couldn't have proof, because I didn't murder anyone."

She set her gloves on the counter near the beaker and nodded. "Now, I'm sure you're ready to leave the Gardens, yes? Jessica was kind enough to bring me back my Death Rose that you found in my office closet, and I have Cerena restrained. She'll be handed over to the proper authorities once I finish my business with you." She reached into the pocket of her lab coat and pulled out a small piece of paper. She handed it to him.

Harvey unfolded it to find a check for fifty-thousand dollars.

"Your payment, detective. Be on your way now. The sun will rise soon, and I have my beautiful plants to attend to."

Harvey set the check on the counter. "You're under arrest."

She rolled her eyes. "By what authority? Yours? You're not an arresting officer. I don't see Midnight City Police Department here. Please, stop spouting nonsense and leave my facility before I have to dispose of you myself."

"You're threatening me?"

She laughed, flashing sharp teeth at him. Though her face revealed her older age, those teeth, that poise, gave off a younger, more hostile vibe. "I don't threaten anyone. I do what I say I will do."

Harvey glanced around the lab. "Where's Jessica?"

Augustine approached one of the rows of planters. She started fiddling with one of the plants—a green leafy one that was set in rich, black soil. "Mr. Elder, you performed your duties as you were commissioned to do. Your business in my Gardens is done. Jessica—and any of the other women who participated in tonight's auction—are not your concern at this point."

Harvey glanced down at the lab counter she had been working at. Papers were scattered all around the counter space around the beakers Augustine had been working with. They looked like nothing more than financial reports and reports on the various plants Augustine was working with within the Gardens.

One paper stuck out to him. A single sheet note that was titled, *Trance Dust Report.*

He glanced up at Augustine, who was still caring to her plants. "Detective, you lost a lot when Lindsay Eves was killed. It wasn't your fault, of course, but you thought it was, and you fell from your high horse as Midnight City's celebrated detective. You lost again when Cynthia left you. That wasn't really any fault of your own either. I don't believe there's a man on this planet that can please that woman. If I were you, I wouldn't tempt fate to see what more you could lose."

With Augustine's back to him, Harvey reached down and slid the sheet of paper off the desk. As Augustine babied her plants, he folded the paper and shoved it into his back pocket.

"Leave, now. This is your last warning. My plants are already attuned to your pheromones. They regard you as hostile and will react in such a way. You may think it seems unnatural, even fantastical that they should act in this manner. They're plants, right? Well, Mr. Elder, plants are living species. And they can be programmed in such a way to protect those that care for them.

"Leave."

Harvey moved past her, making his way toward the foyer hallway. His heart beat fast. He knew she was up to something, knew she was playing a game with him. But to what end?

He reached the doorway expecting some kind of trick or trap. But none awaited him. He pushed on the door and it opened to the foyer hallway.

"Goodbye, detective. I hope Midnight City treats you as well as you've treated the Gardens."

Harvey passed into the hallway. The door slammed shut behind him.

He started down the hallway, glancing at the floral posters along the wall to his right. It seemed so long ago he had arrived here…arrived into the midst of glamour and beauty, knowing nothing of what this night would hold.

He reached the foyer. The hallway continued further along, toward the admin office in front of him. To his left, the sealed door that led outside to the Garden stood, mocking him. To his right, the double doors led to the lobby, his escape.

Tina was trapped in the gardens. He had to help her before he could go anywhere. If he left to get help, she would surely be dead by the time he came back. Augustine acted as if she was doing him a favor by letting him go. He was doing *her* a favor by not restraining her on the spot.

But if he wanted to get Tina to safety, he had to get back into the gardens.

Harvey approached the sealed door. A control panel was built into the right side, but the LCD panel was glowing red. The number keypad had been smashed up, with some of the keypad numbers scattered on the floor, wires and guts spewing forth from the machinery.

He took a deep breath, trying to push back the panic that was intent on seeping in. He reached to his back pocket and took out the paper he had stolen from Augustine's workspace.

Trance Dust Report
After much research and lab tests, I have managed to merge properties

of the Deadly Nightshade and a type of poppy unique only to Midnight City, creating a type of trance-like drug when the ground form of the night-shade root interacts with this poppy. I have found applying the nightshade dust to the surface of the poppy's petals—and then leaving the bloom with-in extremely close vicinity of the test subject—seems to be the most effective, making the recipient malleable and open to full coercion, without any memory of the occurrence. The subject does become docile and will even start to reminisce about the past.

This research has resulted in a few very sick individuals winding up in the hospital—test subjects, as they were—however, no permanent damage was caused by these tests, and the subjects apparently had little to no memory the next day of the trials they underwent, which included requests by me to have them retrieve certain items from the store, from a field, and performing specific duties, such as basic chores.

I have developed an antidote to this concoction, which will return the individual back to a state of lucidity. This antidote is called Perezine—a mixture that I created through years of research for opium poisoning.

I fully back the manufacturing and distribution of this 'trance dust' for use within the Order of the Vine, and other underground organizations that have the funds to purchase from me.

Augustine Rose

Harvey ran his hand through his hair. *So that's how she con-trolled Cerena! Auburn and Tina were right—Cerena wouldn't kill any-one. Not on her own, anyway.*

He folded the note and stuck it back into his pocket. *More proof.*

He looked again at the sealed door leading to the gardens, realizing with grim despair that he wasn't going to be able to help Tina. Not immediately, anyway. He would have to leave and come back with help.

He burst through the double doors into the lobby area.

The lights were out. In darkness, the lobby was much more sinister looking. The posters, the furniture, the lone display of the glowing Twilight Tulip. These items sat, staring at him, watching him.

He passed through the glass doors leading outside. The cold air hit him, and he tightened his overcoat. He looked at the massive flytraps as he made his way along the path leading to the parking lot. The plants seemed to stare at him, but none of them snapped at him or tried to eat him. No, the Venus flytraps made no move against him, but they seemed to warn him not to come back, to forget he had ever stepped foot in this place. To leave Tina and the mystery behind.

To leave Jessica behind.

Sorry, I'm not very good at following directions. Especially from plants.

Rain puddles, scattered around the lot, gave the appearance of blemishes. Harvey counted the vehicles in the lot and came back with the same number that had been here when he first arrived—eight.

That meant that Marigold had *not* driven away from the Gardens, even if she had left, as Tina and Auburn had claimed.

He scanned the lot and noticed a dark shadow lying in the middle of two vehicles—a yellow Jeep and a cherry-red convertible. He cautiously approached it. As he drew closer, he recognized the yellow gown, the ebony skin, the thin figure of Marigold.

Her body was face-down in a rain puddle, and she wasn't moving. A lead pipe rested a few feet from her. Harvey rushed to her side, wary of the rest of the lot. If someone had ambushed her, they could still be out here. Cerena, Jessica, even Augustine—three people he still had to be on his guard for.

Her dress was soaked in rainwater. He pulled on her arm, turning her over. Her mask was shattered, and a bloody wound sat in her face where her left eye and her nose would be. Feeling for a pulse, Harvey confirmed she was dead.

Her purse was still looped around her arm. He gently lifted her limb and pulled her purse off it.

He dumped the contents on the ground in front of him: the letter from her friend, Stephany, lipstick, a compact, a bottle of the liquor Harvey was inspecting at the bar earlier, a stack of cash, and a brown envelope with the wax seal broken—two hands with ivy circling them. The Order of the Vine.

He took the document and ran to his car, unlocking it with his keys before sliding into the driver's seat. He slammed the door shut, locked it, and then sat there in his car with the retrieved item.

He opened the envelope and pulled out a single document:

Vine Missive

Flora Rose,

If you decide to pursue your personal vengeance against Cerena Hatcher, you have the blessings of The Order. This must be a solid frame-up. We can have nothing connecting you to her crime, because then the crime can be traced back to The Order. If you want to test out your latest concoction in this particular instance, I suggest doing so. You can use the Death Rose and Cerena's love of Victor to kill him. If it works, The Order will consider full distribution of your trance dust in our established drug lines. May nature shine upon you, child.

Nightmother

Nightmother? He had heard of The Nightmother in certain circles within the Underground of Midnight City. She was feared, mostly by drug dealers and the criminal class. She gained notoriety years ago when she was rumored to be responsible for establishing an entire network of plant-based drugs that eventually poisoned their users, leading to the death of five thousand people collectively, between Midnight City and other cities the drugs had been distributed to.

He put the letter on the front passenger seat and took a deep breath before shoving the key into his ignition. He would have to get to a phone. He had a few places he could go to for that. Then the police would have to act quickly, bring the hammer down on this place if they wanted any chance of finding Tina alive.

He glanced in his side mirror, which, as usual, was stuck in the down position, giving him a glimpse at a rain puddle. A red blinking light caught his eye.

A bomb.

He slowly pulled his key out of the ignition, mostly sure that it was the starting of the engine that would trigger the explosive.

Harvey carefully pulled on the door handle and opened the driver's side door, his eyes watching the Gardens and the parking lot around him. If Augustine wanted to kill him, she could have used a remote bomb. That meant she was probably watching him right now, waiting to press a little red button and blow him to pieces.

Harvey grabbed the letter from the passenger seat and then chanced it, stepping out of the car. His feet splashed into the puddle near his tire as he broke out in a run, away from the car, taking refuge on the other side of the parking lot, behind the red convertible.

He waited, expecting the explosion to follow.

But nothing happened.

Ignition triggered, he thought.

He realized the only way to end all of this was to put a stop to Augustine. To find Jessica. And bring justice to the Gardens.

Chapter 24

The explosion rocked the ground he stood on, lighting up the darkness that snuck through the earth before dawn. The sound echoed throughout the emptiness surrounding the Gardens, rattling the walls, the glass, the plants.

Harvey watched as his car exploded into a fireball, chunks of the vehicle soaring into the air like metal misshapen birds. The heat from the blast coursed through the lot, reaching him from the cover he took behind the convertible. He felt fire scorch the air, and the cold, dampness that the rain had brought was lit up in an instant, replaced with searing warmth that made it difficult to get a proper gasp of air.

He bent down behind the vehicle, conserving his breath for the precious few moments his mode of transportation was transformed into nothing more than a flaming pile of debris. He had managed to fiddle with the wiring of the car and set a timed ignition. Something he learned in his earlier days when he had to know how to carjack a vehicle.

Minutes passed, and Harvey finally peered over the convertible to see nothing but a charred framework of his car. Though he had had a love/hate relationship with the Datsun, it had, in the end, become a friend to him. Seeing it now in ruins, he felt dismay and sadness.

But when he saw the doors of the Gardens open and saw Augustine briskly make her way down the pathway leading to the parking lot, he grinned. He could finally put a stop to this once and for all.

He watched as she approached the flaming wreckage. Harvey had seen villains in his life, people who became subhuman through their actions against others or through their intentions to seek and consume power. He had seen the worst humanity had to offer, but never had he seen the smile that came over Augustine's face.

In the firelight, her grin struck fear into Harvey's heart. Her jowls lit up, like those of an ancient cryptid, part beast and part human, but all sinister.

He broke free from the fear that seemed to grip him so easily, and he ran behind the watching flytraps back to the main building.

He moved through the front doors, passed through the dark lobby, and wound up in the foyer again.

The doorway to the gardens had been reopened. Auburn's body was gone, and the gazebo out in the distance was lit up like a beacon once again with garden lights and a lit firepit.

He rushed down the hallway, reaching the laboratory door—which was lit green, surprisingly.

Stepping into the laboratory, he listened closely for the sounds of any survivors of this mess. Where was Jessica? Tina? Cerena? As far as he knew, they were still alive somewhere on the premises. It might be up to him to—

"Mr. Elder."

He spun around to find Jessica standing behind him.

He went toward her to pull her to him but stopped mid-action when he saw the Glock in her hand, pointed right at him. A 27 model. The shot would seriously wound or kill him.

"What are you doing, Jessica?" he said, putting his hands up. "I came back here to get you. We have to get—"

She shook her head. "You betrayed...her. Us. The Gardens."

Harvey did a quick glance to his left and right. The lab counter Augustine had been sitting at earlier was to his left, the various antidotes and liquid mixtures. To his right was a wall of vines where Cerena and Tina were restrained and unconscious.

"Were you part of this the whole time?"

She tilted her head. It was then that he noticed the small corsage on the breast of her white cardigan. The Bewitching Poppy.

"Jessica. You're being duped. I need you to listen to me, okay? I need you to come back to me."

Jessica pulled the slide on the gun and pointed it straight at his face. "Mr. Elder, you've served your purpose here in the Gardens. It's time to...remove...you."

He shook his head.

"I gave you the chance to leave, detective."

Augustine appeared from the shadows behind Jessica.

"It's fascinating, isn't it. The power of plants? So many people—ignorant people—such as yourself, take for granted the phenomenal power of the flora in Midnight City. This traitor brought you into my little game, and for that, the both of you will pay."

He slid his hands in the pockets of his coat, realizing this could very well be it.

His right hand felt an object in his pocket—a vial. One he hadn't put there.

Augustine glanced at the sketches above her lab desk. "You

don't understand how much time and energy and money I have invested in this place. So, you wouldn't understand what I will do to protect it. Not just from the likes of you, but from the likes of Jessica. From the likes of those women who died in the Gardens." She motioned to Cerena and Tina who were strapped to the vine wall. "And these two. Cerena will go to prison for the death of my husband. And Tina will return to her life with the promise of compensation for keeping her mouth shut about all of this.

"The Gardens, detective, will be protected. Protected from that undercover snitch, Winter. Protected by traitors, such as Jessica here. And protected from rogue heroes, such as yourself."

The front door of the lab suddenly slammed shut. Augustine turned to see what the commotion was, and Harvey used the brief distraction to pull the vial from his pocket. The label said Perezine. He unscrewed the cap and splashed the vial into Jessica's face. She stumbled back and pulled the trigger of the gun, firing a bullet directly at Harvey. He lunged to the right, but the bullet clipped his left shoulder and sent him backwards to the floor. The impact of the cement on the back of his head nearly knocked him out.

Augustine swung to attack Jessica, but she was flailing around too much, firing shots of the gun off with one hand while she scratched at the liquid in her face with the other.

Harvey pulled himself behind one of the planter racks, hoping it would shield him from the random bullet play. He gripped his shoulder, feeling a tear in his overcoat and a wet stain of blood where he had been clipped. Pain blossomed through his arm. He looked down at the wound and realized the bullet had exited out the back of his shoulder.

Bullets shattered glass vials, penetrated thick soil, and ricocheted off pieces of metal. Harvey knew the .40 caliber bullets would kill him or any of the others in the room if they struck the right place.

The firing stopped. He peered around the corner of the planter rack and watched as Jessica lifted the gun toward Augustine.

Augustine put her hands up. "Jessica. Take it easy. Calm down, now."

Harvey stood up and came out from behind his cover. He put his good hand out to Jessica. "Jessica. Take it easy. Give me the gun."

She stared at him, the whites of her eyes speckled with orange dots, and her breathing labored. She pointed the gun at the floor and hunched over. "What happened?"

Augustine slid behind Jessica and put her hand on the gun, lifting Jessica's arm toward Harvey. "Just pull the trigger. Let it all fall into place."

Jessica pulled free from Augustine's grip and spun around so the gun was pointed at her own chest. "What are you doing? What is going on?"

"Don't do it, Augustine," Harvey said. "We can work this out. There's no reason to kill Jessica."

Augustine smirked. "Of course there isn't, detective. Sometimes we don't need reasons for the things we do. Only desire." She pulled the trigger as Jessica screamed.

But no bang echoed through the lab. No bullet left the gun. Because there were no bullets left.

Harvey pulled Jessica toward him and placed her behind him as he faced Augustine. "No more bullets," he said, smiling. He grabbed Augustine's arm and ripped the gun out of her other hand. "We're done with all of this. You're under arrest for the murder of Winter Jackson, Haylie Wilds, and Auburn Simpson."

Augustine frowned. "You really think any of your charges are going to stick? You have no bodies, detective. You have no proof."

"I'll witness against you," Jessica snapped as she pulled the corsage off her blouse and threw it to the floor. "After all these years, I helped you build the Gardens, and you resort to murdering people? For murdering Cerena because she cheated with your husband?"

Augustine huffed. "You of the lower class would know nothing of our world, child. I let you in to give you a glimpse of what could be. You turned traitor when you called this riff raff in here to interrupt my game."

"Don't worry," Harvey said, "you can play plenty of games in prison."

"Not so fast, Harvey."

The voice was familiar. The tone. The pitch. He turned to find Cynthia standing in the doorway to the lab, blocking him from carting Augustine into the hallway. She wore a long, black trench coat, black heels, and her long, black hair was up in a tight, fancy bun.

"Cynthia?"

She smiled, hands in the pockets of her coat. "I had a feeling you would solve the case."

Augustine turned to Cynthia. "Cynthia. You understand you're interrupting a Nightmother Missive?"

Cynthia moved no part of her body but her eyes, which she focused squarely on Augustine. "I am fully aware of what I'm doing."

"What's going on here," Harvey said. Jessica moved to his side.

"You're here because of me, Harvey," Cynthia said. "Geez, Harvey. I help you get one case and you already have bullet wounds?"

Harvey went to move toward the phone on the lab table, but Cynthia jotted in front of him.

"Hold on. I think there is a *better* way to handle this."

"I have to call the Department. Augustine needs to go away, for a very long time."

Cynthia moved in close to him, her brilliant eyes pleading with him. "Just hear me out, yes?"

He could smell her rose-scented perfume. "How are you involved in all of this?"

"I am involved much more than you'll ever know. What I propose is that you hear me out before calling in the calvary. The deaths here in the Gardens, they are unfortunate. But you must know each of these women is a criminal in their own right." She stepped back and rubbed her hands together before blowing in between them. "Cold in here. Anyway, just think of their deaths as Fate taking out the trash."

"You want me to look the other way on everything I saw tonight?"

Cynthia shook her head. "No, that's ridiculous. I *wanted* you to see all of this, Harvey. I *wanted* you to dig your heels in, to use that brain of yours and figure this whole thing out. I knew you could, but you didn't know you could. Now we're at the end of it, and I would like to offer you the money you were offered—the fifty thousand dollars—plus I'd like to throw a few hundred thousand more on the pile for your...discretion."

"You're trying to buy my silence?"

He felt a hand on his good shoulder and became aware Jessica was standing behind him. "Even if he doesn't say anything, I will."

Cynthia grinned like a Cheshire cat. "Honey, nobody will believe anything you have to say. You know why? Because you were Augustine's right-hand pawn. If I snap my fingers just so, you'll be put in the same cell with her as an accomplice."

"I had nothing to do with this," Jessica growled.

Cynthia tilted her head. "Yeah. You can tell them that all you want, but the police aren't going to believe you."

Harvey nudged Cynthia to the side and went straight for the phone.

"Harvey, this doesn't have to be this complicated."

He dialed out to the Department. He reported the crimes. He was told the VFPD would be at the Gardens in about ten minutes.

As he set the receiver down, Cynthia shook her head. "You live in a dump, Harvey. You live in a dump. You have no car now. Brilliant move, by the way—blowing the car up to get Augustine out of her den of lies. I really enjoyed watching that. Look, you have no real life to speak of. It's time you upgraded. That's all I ever wanted for you, you know? I wanted the best, but for reasons beyond my understanding, I couldn't pull that 'best' out of you."

"Well, here's your chance."

"Did you orchestrate all of this?"

She laughed. "Heavens, no. It's not *all* about you, Harvey. Geez, you have a nice ego there, don't you? No, I have my own reasons for setting all of this up."

Two individuals stepped into the laboratory and looked straight at Cynthia. One was a black female, the other was a white male. They were tall, slender, and each was wearing a black coat and pants, with white shirts underneath.

Cynthia nodded to them, then pointed her finger toward the vine wall where Tina and Cerena were. "Cut them down."

The two strangers nodded and headed to the two restrained women.

"Friends of yours?" Harvey asked as he gripped his

wounded shoulder. The bleeding seemed to have stopped, but the pain was only getting worse.

Cynthia stared him in the eyes. "You could say that. Anyway, Harvey, you need to understand one thing about me. You knew nothing about me. I know, that probably wasn't fair to you. I didn't leave you just because you couldn't pull your life together, but also because I have aspirations that go beyond your moral aptitude."

"Crime."

She tilted her head left, then right. "You call it what you will. Listen, the police are going to arrive. Augustine will be charged with her husband's murder. The Trance Dust operation here will be shut down. Cerena and Tina will be set free. They are…associates of mine…anyway."

Augustine laughed. "Shut down the Trance Dust Operation and you sever your ties to the Nightmother. You'll be excommunicated."

Cynthia turned to Augustine and patted her cheek. "So naïve and clueless. *You're* the one who botched up the Trance Dust Operation. Once Harvey called the police, they found everything of yours—the lab, the materials, the drugs. You screwed it all up. You'll be in prison a while, and you'll be the one excommunicated."

Augustine's countenance dropped.

Cynthia smiled at Harvey. "The Order of the Vine is in your debt, Harvey. You successfully retrieved the Death Rose, stopped Augustine Paxton and—"

"Rose," Augustine blurted out.

Cynthia rolled her eyes. "And her plans to destroy the Order. And you saved the lives of Cerena Hatcher and Tina Redfield. I'd say you're a detective through and through."

Cynthia's associates returned to her, each propping Cerena and Tina up.

"We'll take them with us," Cynthia said. "We'll clean them up and administer any help they need. I'm sure they don't want to be here when the police arrive."

Cerena groaned, her eyes focusing on Harvey. "You saved me?"

He nodded.

Tina shook Cynthia's associate—the women—off of her. Then she stepped forward toward Harvey. "I appreciate you, detective. You may have saved my life out there. I too am in your debt." She slipped something into Harvey's hand.

He looked down and found a small pin, a circle of vines with the outstretched hands in the center.

Cynthia raised an eyebrow. "Don't lose that, detective. She just put herself in your debt. For anything."

Tina nodded, her eyes sparkling at him. "Anything." She and Cerena left with Cynthia's associates.

Harvey slid the pin into his jacket pocket.

Cynthia checked her watch. "I have to leave now, Harvey. Sorry to leave you twice in a month. This time, however, you're a much stronger person. I believe, anyway. Call me if you need the Order's help, yes? Don't be shy about that. Just don't call me anymore for a date."

"Don't worry," he said.

"Oh, and here." She plunged her hands in her pockets and pulled out Harvey's phone, lockpick kit, and dusting kit. "These belong to you."

He took the items, happy to have them back. He put them in his pocket, nestled near the wrapped gun he still had. The one with Cerena's prints.

Cynthia nodded. "Good luck, detective. And get that wound cleaned up." She left the lab, vanishing into the hallway beyond.

Moments later, the police arrived, taking Augustine into custody.

Chapter 25

I nspector Reins approached Harvey as his officers took Augustine out of the building. Harvey now had a bandage underneath his shirt, wrapped around his left shoulder where the bullet had struck him. Luckily, the bullet had passed all the way through, leaving a nasty wound but making it to where it would heal alright. Not to mention how it had ruined Harvey's favorite coat.

"Detective—Harvey—the story you and your," Inspector Reins pointed to Jessica who sat next to him at the foyer bar, "associate here are telling us seems a bit unbelievable. Haunted plants?"

"Not haunted," Harvey replied. Though he didn't know what to call them.

Jessica let out a light breath. "I know it seems crazy, but it's all part of Augustine's experiments. You'll find them all out there, in the Gardens."

Inspector Reins pointed out the open doorway to the gardens. "Those gardens?"

Harvey nodded. "What other gardens do you see around here?"

Inspector Reins chuckled. "There's nothing out there but a

bunch of plants. Most of them dead."

"What?" Harvey stood up from the barstool, gazing out onto the purple pathway and the gazebo out in the center. Now that he looked closely, he saw that all of the plants in the gardens seemed not brown and withered, but greyscale, lacking any color. Void of life.

Police had been unable to find the bodies of Winter Jackson, Auburn Simpson, or Haylie Wilds. Harvey and Jessica had recounted their time at the Gardens at least twice now—once for one of the detectives who had come and gone, and a second time for Inspector Reins.

Neither believed their stories.

Inspector Reins approached the open doorway. The sun was starting to break across the horizon, leaking liquid sunlight across the cracked sky. "Nothing here. We investigated the fountain—nothing. No invisible plants. No signs of a Maddening Magnolia or a Death Rose. We found posters and mentions of these plants around the grounds, but that's about it.

"The laboratory turned up the Trance Dust that Augustine had been concocting. That stuff has been turned over to the ATF. One of the biggest—most unusual—drug busts they've had in a while. We found physical evidence of Augustine stabbing and killing her husband. He was in fact the victim we found on the other side of the city. We found nothing more really that would indicate any of the other strange events you and your girlfriend here indicated to me in your debriefing."

Harvey scratched the stubble on his jaw. It felt like sandpaper. "I gave you the Nightmother Missive. The Trance Dust Report."

Inspect Reins nodded. "Yes, you did. They do nothing more really than shed light on Augustine's motives. Certainly implicates her in things."

"What about the Nightmother? The Order of the Vine?"

He waved Harvey's words away, like they were annoying flies buzzing around his face. "Myth. Fantasy. Nothing more."

Jessica approached the men. Harvey noticed her eyes were cleared up from the orange speckles, but her hair was a tangled mess. "It's all true, Inspector. I have paperwork in the office that can—"

Inspector Reins waved her away as he started toward the lobby doors. "Yes, I saw all of it. It simply connects Augustine to these women you say went missing."

"Were murdered," Harvey corrected.

Inspector Reins turned to both of them. "I found nothing that could be used as evidence of the three 'dead' women. I have evidence to link Augustine to her husband's murder."

"But those women—"

"Nothing, detective." He shrugged. "*Nothing.*" Inspector Reins strolled through the lobby doors, leaving Harvey and Jessica alone in the foyer.

The cold morning air, tinted with the scent of rain, poured into the building, prompting Harvey to pull his coat closed.

Jessica looked up at him, her eyes tired, her smile waning. "What now?"

"It's obvious Inspector Reins has been paid off by Cynthia, no doubt to protect the Order of the Vine."

Jessica nodded. "Figures."

Harvey took a deep breath. Remnants of the floral scent that had once permeated the Gardens wafted around them, like the spirit of the now-dead garden coming through to taunt them.

"Maybe we could go get some breakfast? Together?"

Harvey thought about that for a moment, then nodded. "Sure. That would be nice."

He felt his phone ring in his pocket. He pulled it out and answered, giving a sidelong glance to Jessica, who just stood, staring out at the corpse of what was once the Gardens.

"Hello," he said.

"Is this Harvey Elder?" a woman's voice asked. The tone was nasally. *"Detective Harvey Elder?"*

He took a deep breath. "Yeah. Who wants to know?"

"Mr. Elder, my name is Stacey. I'm one of the workers down here at Dark Grounds. I...I found your number on her phone."

He felt his heart stop for a second. "Whose phone?"

"Monique. Monique Ball."

He took a deep breath and turned away from Jessica. "Monique? What happened to her?"

The woman sniffled into the phone, then cleared her throat before blowing her nose. Harvey waited impatiently.

"You need to come down here, detective. Someone kidnapped my friend. The police say they have no proof someone took her, that it hasn't been long enough for a missing persons report. But I want to hire you to find her. To find my friend."

His voice almost caught in his throat at the thought of anyone kidnapping or otherwise harming Monique. "I'll be right down there."

"Please hurry."

Harvey disconnected the call and turned to Jessica. "Looks like I'll have to take a raincheck on that breakfast date."

Jessica nodded. "I understand. I should probably go home and rest."

"Could you drop me somewhere on your way home?"

She nodded, a very faint sparkle glistening in her eye. "Yeah, I can do that. Detective."

Detective Harvey Elder will return in *Hotel Arbor*, a Midnight City mystery coming 2025!

About the Author

Born at the tail end of the 70's, David reveled in the pop culture of the 80's and 90's, building his childhood around the success of Star Wars, the jokes of Ace Ventura, and the adventure of *The Goonies*. His passion for writing began in the early 90's, and he finished his first novel when he was 16. With the death of his grandmother - who was his biggest fan - he stopped writing and sought adventure, traveling constantly between California and Arizona as he fought to find a purpose while also walking the long-winding, and incredibly narrow, trail of faith.

Decades later, he found himself in Arizona, with a passion to write once again.

David is the author of The Black Earth Series, The Expired Reality Series, and The Midnight City Series, among other stories.